Praise for

"With **The Coyote Bead**, Gerald Hausman once again displays the sensitivity and sympathetic understanding toward Native people that has long marked his work. This novel offers an intriguing look into a tragic and—unjustly—little-known episode in American history; younger readers of all races should enjoy it."

—William Sanders
award-winning science fiction author of *Journey to Fusang*

"More than a poignant tale, more than a story laced with native magic, **The Coyote Bead** is steeped in the richness of Navajo legends which prove determination and perseverance can bring ultimate triumph to all those who have the courage to believe in themselves."

—Mary Summer Rain, author of *The Singing Web*

"Gerald Hausman brings a poet's keen vision to this narrative of a Native American tragedy, one that reverberates with so much that was to come in our own time. Hausman knows the Navajo people, the land, and the healing wisdom of their culture as well as any living American writer."

—Aram Saroyan, author of *Day and Night: Bolinas Poems*

"Once again Gerald Hausman has delivered a powerful book for a new generation of readers who deserve to know the whole truth of the past. The tragic yet poignant story of a band of resolute Navajo people as told in **The Coyote Bead** is as timeless and provocative as the account of the Joads in *The Grapes of Wrath*. This is an important story of human struggle, resiliency, and hope."

—Michael Wallis, author of *The Real Wild West*

Praise for Books by Gerald Hausman

"Gerald Hausman's *Tunkashila* is an eloquent tribute to the first great storytellers of America."

—*The New York Times Book Review*

"He feels the flying horse manes and the lingering spirits which speak in those winds which touch the trees."

—Charles Dailey, The Institute of American Indian Arts

"*Tunkashila* is a book to read slowly and with deep respect . . . it is like the wind one hears on the plains, steady, running, full of music."

—N. Scott Momaday, author of *The House Made of Dawn*

On *The Gift of the Gila Monster*: " . . . His examination of the ceremonial stories of this remarkable people . . . is a revealing sample, astutely selected."

—Tony Hillerman, author of *Coyote Waits*

Books by Gerald Hausman

Navajo Nights

Meditations with Animals:
A Native American Bestiary

The Kebra Negast: [The Book of Rastafarian Wisdom
and Faith from Ethiopia and Jamaica]

Tunkashila:
From the Birth of Turtle Island to the Blood of Wounded Knee

The Gift of the Gila Monster

Books Written with Loretta Hausman

The Mythology of Dogs:
Canine Legend and Lore through the Ages

The Mythology of Cats:
Feline Legend and Lore through the Ages

Dogs of Myth: Tales from Around the World
(illustrated by Barry Moser)

The Coyote Bead

Gerald Hausman

HAMPTON ROADS
PUBLISHING COMPANY, INC.

Cover design by Mayapria Long
Cover Art Courtesy of Charles Dailey, The Institute of American
Indian Arts Museum, Santa Fe, New Mexico
Interior art by Mariah Fox and Jay DeGroat

For information write:

Hampton Roads Publishing Company, Inc.
134 Burgess Lane
Charlottesville, VA 22902

Or call: 804-296-2772
FAX: 804-296-5096
e-mail: hrpc@hrpub.com
Web site: http://www.hrpub.com

If you are unable to order this book from your local
bookseller, you may order directly from the publisher.
Quantity discounts for organizations are available.
Call 1-800-766-8009, toll-free.

Library of Congress Catalog Card Number: 99-71609

ISBN 1-57174-145-3

10 9 8 7 6 5 4 3 2 1

Printed on acid-free paper in Canada

Author's Note

A long time ago, they came out of the earth and called themselves *Dineh,* "The People." So the old stories tell us.

Dineh lived on the tabletopped plateaus and in the canyon lands of the great Southwest. Nomadic, they moved where they wanted, but they believed that wherever they set foot, that ground was holy. Every mountain and river was sacred, each shining fleck of sunstruck quartz, each blade of grass arching in the sun—all were part of the pantheon of the gods.

In the passage of time, *Dineh* hunted, farmed, and herded sheep in the country known as the Four Corners—where New Mexico, Arizona, Utah, and Colorado meet. Yet, though they were stationary, *Dineh* roamed all over, raiding whites and Indians alike. And they were feared from one end of Four Corners to the other.

From the Pueblos *Dineh* took women, children, clothing, blankets, and horses. From the Spanish they stole silver and the art of making jewelry, which they did far better than their predecessors. They were ruthless and free, and the hills resounded with tales of their comings and goings; and legends came of this. And their storytellers wrought ancient tales of conquest and adventure, and retold them to fit the times.

Then came the blue coats—as they were called by *Dineh.* The white eyes, *'eyoni,* or "Enemy People." These were the soldiers wearing dark blue uniforms who fought against The People, and eventually confiscated their lands, burned their peach trees, and scattered their flocks of sheep.

In the end, The People surrendered to the American government, for whom the blue coats were orderlies. Afterwards, *Dineh* went on a forced march of 350 miles to Fort Sumner in southeastern New Mexico. There, they suffered and died. There, they fell prey to illness and famine, their numbers dwindling, until they were reduced to a few thousand.

Today The People still talk about "The Long Walk," as they have named it. They remember the whole amazing, debilitating tragedy, as if it had happened yesterday. Particularly, they recall the American Indian bounty hunters that turned them in to the blue coat soldiers. Their bitterest enemy was the Ute tribe, and this enmity stretches far back into their mythology, as well as their contemporary history.

When stories are swapped on the Reservation even now, the names of certain Ute enemies are mentioned along with the routinely despised, all-American hero, Kit Carson. However, the most diabolical nemesis of *Dineh*—so say the storytellers—wasn't a human being. He was a monster, a myth, a man—a tragicomic deity named Coyote. There is a ceremony to tame him, to bring him under control. It is known as the Coyote Beadway. How it came into existence is mysterious, a thing lost in time. According to Bluejay (Joogii) DeGroat, whose father was a medicine man, the narrative of the Coyote Beadway tells how a warring nation, the Navajo, were changed into the strong, peaceful people of the present time. Today, they are one of the largest indigenous cultures in the United States.

The tale of The Coyote Bead belongs to Jay and to his father, who helped each of us to understand it. We retell The Coyote Bead now with his blessing. We humbly dedicate it to his father's memory and to those Navajo friends with whom we lived and shared fry bread over the last three decades: Rae Joe, Jimmy BlueEyes, Ray Brown, Ray Tsosie, Ramos Tsosie, Loren White Straight Eagle Plume, and especially, Joogii.

Into the Cool Dark Air

Canyon del Muerto, Arizona, 1864

There were rumors of war before the first frost of autumn. But they were only rumors, and we saw no enemies except the usual bands of Utes, coming and going, as they always did. We didn't see the one called Two Face, the man with the scar, who was their leader. We just saw a lot of blue coats, milling around in different camps. But they did not come over to our canyon and they left us alone.

My father said, "Maybe they don't want to fight."

But Grandfather asked him, "Do you think they have come here to camp?"

That day, my parents were killed.

This is how it happened.

First, I should tell you my name. I am called Tobachischin and my grandfather is called Dinneh-Kloth, but these are formal and we seldom use them. I have not told you the names of my mother and father because they were murdered by the blue coats. It is impolite to speak of the dead, and I will not do it. But I can tell you that I was born into my mother's clan, the people of the salt. And, my father's clan, the water people. My name, Tobachischin, means Water's Child. Tobachischin is a great name because that person was the Sun Father's son; but that is another story, for another time.

My mother was stirring a pot of peaches at the time I heard the hoofbeats echo on the canyon walls. Father was away, deer hunting, when the blue coats came up on their horses. A man who rode in front and had very dirty yellow hair spoke in American to my mother, "This will be your last meal." There were twenty men, in all. The horses stamped and pawed at the soft, red sand as the man talked. We understood his language, but we didn't usually let on that we could speak it. There was no sound except the licking of the flames and the nervous hooves of the horses.

The blue coat leader with the yellow hair wiped his forehead with the cloth that white people use to store their sweat and nose particles. He looked annoyed, not worried.

"There is a place we're going to take you," the man said. "You call it *Hweeldi*. That is where we're going to take you."

My mother did not look up from her constant stirring. The juniper smoke, blue and faint in the white sunlight, drifted.

My mother, not looking away from the fire, asked in Navajo, "Why are you here? You don't belong here."

The blue coat took off his blue cap. He ran his finger around the inside of the brim. His hair was the color of corn silk, dirty yellow. His teeth, when he spoke, were gray. I remembered that Grandfather said people with gray teeth were the relations of Gray Giant, the monster who was killed by Coyote in the beginning time. Gray Giant also had yellow hair. So, I knew this man couldn't be trusted, and that he had to be evil.

However, my mother made no sign that she knew any of these things. She stirred the peach stew and I could tell she was thinking. Then my father came out of the bush known as Apache plume. He was leading his big roan horse, on top of which there was a freshly killed deer.

The blue coat never answered my mother's question, but now he asked my father, "Why are you carrying that buck on your horse? Don't you know you won't have any use for it at *Hweeldi*?"

My father said nothing, nor did his face show any surprise. I heard a hawk cry, somewhere far off in the upper canyon. It was answered by a little wren.

The blue coat turned and addressed the men on horseback.

"I don't think these people understand American," he said.

A small, fat, shuffling Navajo came out from behind the snorting horses. He walked slowly, his mouth open. He looked ugly.

He addressed my mother in Navajo.

"What are you doing?"

She didn't answer.

The air began to smell sweetly of stewing peaches.

"What you're doing is foolish," the Navajo said. His pants could not contain his belly. He wore a torn old vest. His clothes were made of cloth and they were threadbare and you could see his knees, which were dark brown from the sun.

I glanced at my father to see what he might be thinking. He was calm, and very still. Holding the reins of his roan, he watched to see what would happen. His deer rifle was in his right hand, the reins were in his left. The big red horse, standing in the sun with the dead buck heavy upon it, cast a shadow over my father. He was entirely in that shadow, unmoving and calm.

"That is a foolish thing you are doing," the fat man said, sneering.

"What did you say?" asked the yellow-hair soldier.

The fat man, ignoring him, went on.

"There will be no peaches on the long walk to *Hweeldi*. On the long walk, you will have nothing to eat and you will die. What good is food to the dead?"

The fragrance of the peaches hung on the air.

The blue cedar smoke lay in the windless space between the canyon walls.

The yellow-hair man told the fat Navajo to stop talking.

No one said anything.

No one moved.

What my father did then was unseen because he was mostly in shadow. He dropped to his knees, and levering a shell into his rifle, he fired from the hip. A spurt of flame came out of the barrel of his gun. The fat Navajo fired back at him with a pistol.

Suddenly, there were many guns going off all around me. I ran to shield my mother, but a bullet stung my ankle. Another caught my mother in the neck. She dropped beside the stewpot, dead. In the little thicket of Apache plume, my father disappeared. His rifle spat flame, the blue coats went to their bellies or behind their horses. There hadn't been any time for them to retreat and they were firing wildly, centering their shots at the thicket where my father was hidden. I was lying beside my mother, trying to keep myself flat. The bullets were kicking up dust and ringing against the canyon walls.

Then, all at once, no sound came from the Apache plume. In this moment of quiet, I knew my father had joined my mother. His big red horse was still standing in the sunlight, with the buck heavy upon it. I touched my ankle and felt cold blood. I didn't know if I could run, but I was going to try. In the confusion, the yellow-hair soldier had spun around on his horse, shooting at my father. There was a cloud of fine red dust where his horse stirred it up, and I stood up and, using this as cover ran for the crack in the canyon, where we stored our valuable things.

Running, I stumbled twice. No shots were fired. I made it to the crack. The blue coats stopped firing. I vanished into the fissure in the canyon wall, and fell into the cool dark air.

The Long Journey Home

I was in a narrow place. The sheer stone on either side of me was so high, it nearly shut out the sky. The bullet in my right ankle throbbed and hummed, and I was stumbling. Yet my arms were strong and they would carry me up the yucca-plaited ladder to the table-top above. This was the way Grandfather had gone earlier that morning. It was where he lived, safe from the Utes, the Spanish, and now, these blue coats.

I would join him up there, if I could.

Listening, I waited.

The sound of crunching boots, stomping hooves. A horse's neigh. A clapping sound, whistling. Then, silence. After a while, I heard the canyon wren's song, saying all is well.

I put my hands on the old, old rope ladder. The braiding was well worn, but strong. Gripping it tightly, I started my ascent. I had to drag my leg along, my moccasin full of wet blood. There would be a trail of it, yet, once the ladder was pulled up after me, nobody could follow. Up top, among the clouds, I would be safe. I climbed.

Surely, Grandfather was waiting for me. I glanced up, expecting to see the curve of his head, his white hair. I didn't see anything, though, except the flare of pink rock. The sun was peeking into the crack, turning dim blue to red gold. I made for that light, hauling my bleeding leg.

Almost there, resting on a little ledge, I saw an owl. Blinking, it flew dazed into a shaft of sunlight, ruffling the quiet air and buffeting my face with wings of dry dust. I smelled the owl after he'd gone and I shivered. Owls are usually scary, messengers from the Land of the Dead. Was I going to die?

Forcing myself up, I climbed ever higher. My bad leg dangled, dripping, useless. Down the pretty pink rock went my life's blood, staining the cliff face maroon. There were notches in the wall, footholds carved long ago by the Anasazi, our old enemy ancestors, as we call them.

I braced my good leg, setting my foot into the notch, and rested. The floor of the canyon was a thin brown, sand-colored ribbon far below me. Above, almost within reach, was the sunlit shelf that marked the end of my climb.

A strange feeling came over me. I was sweating, but my skin was cold. My throat was dry and it hurt to swallow. I could feel the blood on my ankle, the dripping. But no pain any more. Inside my chest my heart hammered and I heard a deep, dull thud in my ears. An icy feeling was moving up my chest like winter water.

The dryness in my throat burned. I kept thinking,

soon I will be able to drink. The summer rains had filled the high cavities in the mesas with much good water. Yesterday, it had rained. The water was there, if I could get to it, but now my arms were shaking. I put all of my weight on my left leg and wearily dragged myself up the last of the ladder's length.

Then I made one last great effort so that I lay, straight out, on the rock shelf above the crack in the canyon. I'd made it. My eyelids flickered in the bright sun. Where was Grandfather? Shouldn't he have been here by now? Hadn't he heard the shooting?

The sky roof of the canyon started to swirl all around me, and I saw the Apache plume and the cliff roses blowing, the sun shining, and I heard the voices of the blue coats in the depths of the canyon echoing.

I dreamed then and I went around like a wagon wheel until I saw the face of the Ute enemy, the one we call *Altsaabinii'i*—"Two Face." His eyes were set very close together, his forehead and nose separated by a reckless scar that ran river-like down to his chin. Once, so they say, one of our men broke his face with an ax, giving him not one but two faces.

In the dream Two Face grinned and his scar snaked across his face, moving with the effort made by his tightening smile. I woke up gasping, short of breath. The smell of smoke crept over the mesa. It didn't have the piercing sharpness of cedar and it smelled sour.

I knew that smell; they were burning our peach trees. The brownish smoke came clotted on the wind and went over me.

I began to crawl in the sun. I saw my mother—in my mind. Then my father. I snapped my eyes shut, closing off the vision of my mother stirring peaches. Closing off forever the picture of my father, fallen in the Apache plume.

If I thought too strongly of them, they could return from the shadow world. They could turn back. That would be bad. Better that I should join them than for them to try and join me.

Where was Grandfather? The burning peach trees offended my nose, reminding me of that stew and the patient hands that stirred it. My troubled mind dimmed, darkened. A tide of blood washed over me, and I was unconscious again.

When I woke I saw that I'd dragged myself to a rock basin full of runoff water. I let my face fall into its coolness. And drank deeply. Some distance away, the crack of rifles. Reminding me of the yucca ladder. Had I forgotten to pull it up after me? Someone could be coming up on it right now. I painfully pushed my face away from the water and wriggled back the way I'd come. I followed my own blood spoor, which had the scent of rust and lichen and dead animals. I continued to drag my broken body back to the edge of the cliff.

The first thing I did when I got there was to plant my elbows on either side of me, in case someone, or something, was waiting for me.

The surprise came so fast; I hadn't time to do anything except strike with my hands. That fat Navajo had hauled himself up the same way I had. His face was risen in front of me like a dirty brown moon. The mustache hairs on either side of his mouth were twitching and his eyes crinkled with the strain of climbing. He was very fat. He was also suspended there, holding the yucca ladder with one hand, while grasping the cliff top with the other.

I struck him then—hard. My fist hit his chin, glancing off. He grabbed my shirt, and held on to it and the cotton shirt tore down the front; I slipped forward and went halfway off the edge. The toes of my left foot hooked into a juniper root, and I grabbed the ladder at the same time.

The fat man let go of my torn shirt when it ripped away and then I saw him reach into his belt for a knife. The glint of the blade winked in the sun, and swiped at my face. The fat man jerked himself up a little bit closer. I let go of the ladder and seized the hand with the knife. Banging his knuckles against the cliff face, I managed to knock the knife free, and it was suddenly in my own hand. Quickly I sawed the loop on the leather ladder-stay, and as it creaked, I saw the fat man snatching at the canyon wall, grabbing at a dead juniper branch. I drew myself backwards, using the wooden ladder peg. Then I hacked at the other stay, and it snapped, sending the fat man on a spiral trip down, down, down. I saw his face staring at me as he fell, his purple mouth gaping like a fish. He spun down into the dark cleft of that narrow place, and landed with a meaty thud. I backed myself away from the cliff edge, and closing my eyes, passed out.

For a long time I lay there, asleep. When my eyes fluttered open, the heat of the day was past. The rock top was bathed in the golden glow of dusk. My body was numb; all pain was gone. Alive, I felt dead. For a moment I wondered where I was, who I was; then I remembered.

Again I thought of my parents—I couldn't help it. By now, I believed, my mother and father were together, walking in the underworld, going to that far country of the North. The long journey home.

Like a Great Silent Blanket

My eyes flickered and the dark world silvered at the edges and grew brighter, bolder. It was a long time before my thoughts began to take shape, and finally to make sense. For quite a while, soft things touched me, then withdrew, leaving me alone.

Butterflies? Moths?

The world I was in was honey-colored and warm.

Was I awake? It didn't feel like a dream. Still, I didn't know where I was, or who I was; I only knew *that* I was.

The soft-winged things came back. Blurry, the honey-warm place grew, clearer, rounder. Then I heard my grandfather singing.

Grandfather?

I remembered. I was hurt. All up and down my right leg, there was terrible, fiery pain. Numbness at my ankle, and my toes. As if I was dead there, but on fire everywhere else. Remembering, it began to come back and the furry, blurry honeycomb that enclosed me was . . . Grandfather's hogan. So, I reasoned, he'd brought me in from the rock where I'd fallen after I cut the rope that suspended the fat man.

Now I remembered: I had been shot in the right leg. I looked around and saw the familiar shape of things that were known to me. Grandfather's eagle wing brushed me on the left leg as he sang. His small *mano* and *metate*, in which crushed herb was mixed, lay beside his folded knee. I heard him singing. The singing was good to hear. I tried to smile, but couldn't.

Grandfather paused.

Then his chant began again. The words were known to me. The healing song of the black ant people. Grandfather was calling for the ants to come and put me together again. He sang,

> *Black ant people, by your smell,*
> *Bring this broken body together.*
> *Here are his feet, here are his toes.*
> *Put them together.*
> *Here is his ankle, put it in place.*

I could see the ants working, carrying the littlest part of the broken-apart man. Bringing back his body hair, his blood vein, making his bones well and whole again. The song told of what happened when Tobachischin, my namesake, was broken apart by lightning, and how the ants restored him, as now, Grandfather was restoring me.

He sang of thunder, how it rose. He sang of lightning—I knew he'd put zigzag lines of white clay on either side of my mouth. I knew I was lying on a sand painting that showed how the ant people were the first beings to come up out of the earth.

Grandfather sang of wind, how it rose. Black wind, white wind, blue wind, yellow wind, glittering wind. How they rose and went about and did good. There was this on my body as well, the coloring of the wind people, streams of blue and yellow wind.

Grandfather's voice rose and fell in his throat and the eagle feather dipped in the wind of legend and touched me all about the leg. And all round me went the wind people, touching and healing. Reminding me that I was named Tobachischin, the son of the sun. Grandfather sang,

> Glittering wind makes the head whole
> Sun makes the eyes whole
> Whirlwind makes the walking power whole.

I don't know how long I lay there with my eyes open and staring. A long time, I suppose. There was no light in Grandfather's hogan except a small flickering fire. The walls of his place were made of loose rock, chinked with mud. The house faced east, towards the rising sun, and I knew that when he was finished singing, he would open the blanket doorway, and let the sun into the hogan. Then he would move me off the sand painting and scatter the little colored crystals to the winds. Return them to Changing Woman, who is Mother Earth.

For now I heard his song. And felt his feather. I also breathed the good-smelling smoke of cedar. Content to watch this smoke spiral up through the smoke hole, I saw a white sharpness. The day was begun; the night of stars was finished. Then the dark north closed all around me, and I heard the voices of *chindi*—"ghosts." Grandfather's feather protector stopped touching me then. He stopped singing. For a moment, he let the ghosts have their way. I couldn't see them, but I could hear them. Then they faded on the morning wind, and again I slept.

When I awoke Grandfather was offering me some broth. It was in a small gourd, which he pressed to my lower lip. I took some and felt its warmth go deeply into me. Looking down at my leg, I saw that it was splinted with two red-peeled cedar sticks and bound with strips of soft deer hide. Otherwise, my legs were bare and I was wearing my breechcloth, and nothing else. A grayish coating covered my ankle—clay and ash, and spider webbing. My back was propped against a willow-woven backrest. I sipped the broth and sighed.

I heard myself say from a long way away, "I heard that song, Grandfather, it was good."

He looked at me, his face unsmiling. Thoughtful, wondering. The little whiskers about his chin, silver. His skin tan and soft and wrinkled. A shaft of sunlight from the open doorway lay across my leg. So, it was morning. A new day. Grandfather was wearing the blue bandanna of trader's cloth. His hair, long and white, hung well below his back. I knew that he had washed it with yucca, for it was very clean and straight.

"I found you lying, stretched out by the cliff wall. Down below, in the slip, was the fat man you killed." He chuckled.

"That was why I heard the *chindi* voices."

He nodded, offered me more broth.

I drank some more. My lips were cracked and dry.

"Was I sick . . . a long time?"

With his right hand he made a fist that went over his flat left hand. The right crossed the left three times, which meant I had slept for three suns. Three whole days had gone by since I was shot.

"I looked for you, couldn't find you. Then I had the fight with the fat man. After that I dropped off asleep."

He set the round gourd by the crackling fire.

Grandfather cleared his throat. "I will tell you what happened, so that you will always know. That fat man, who brought much shame to the people, led the blue coats into our canyon. Now, there is nothing left."

He made the finish sign—two hands, broken apart.

"Those who are not too old, or too weak, or too small have been taken away to *Hweeldi*. There, they will be given terrible water, bad flour, and rotten meat. The people will die as they have died here. Our trees are burned, our flocks killed, our children stabbed with swords. There is nothing left, but just a few of us. Just a few, like yourself and myself. A broken boy, an old man."

His eyes dimmed with tears. He wiped them away.

With his voice soft as ash, he said, "Soon they will scale the walls of this mesa."

"You know this, Grandfather?"

He nodded; his mouth was grim and tight.

"We have one sun, maybe. Then the *Naakaii*, the Mexicans, will return with Two Face. We have many enemies: the *Naakaii*, the Ute, Two Face, and *Bi'ee Lichii'ii*—Kit Carson. They have lots of guns and gunpowder, and they make a lot of smoke. They want to wipe the people off the earth."

"Can they do this, Grandfather?"

I felt my head swimming, coming loose from my body, as if there were two of me in that hogan; one of them floating off somewhere. Then I saw my body propped upright and I saw Grandfather talking to that half-person that was me, while I, myself, was really above the two of us, floating up around the roof beams. Grandfather looked up, as if he felt something there, knew what was happening.

I got dizzy and started to doze off, but I could still hear Grandfather speaking to me, telling me in his ash-sifted voice that the people would live in caves again, that they would go under the earth, that they would turn into birds, that they would crawl away like lizards and snakes. They would not, he said, be wiped from the earth. They would live, and, one day they would be great again. That was how it was, and would be.

I remember, too, that before I dropped back into my body, I heard *chindi* voices, very near Grandfather. They were not calling to me, they were just there somewhere on the mesa, talking among themselves. So many had been killed, so many had died. So many on the long road North whispering of what they knew. They were looking at their hands and their feet and starting to walk away, but then like a great silent blanket the doorway of the east darkened, and I slept. And heard no more voices, living or dead.

His Yellow Eyes upon Me

When the dawn sun cut across the red cliffs, Grandfather helped me to my feet. The hogan wobbled, I felt myself swimming. Grandfather gave me a cedar staff, carved so that it fit comfortably under my arm. Shouldering my weight on to my left side, I struggled out into the sun. The blood rushed to my ankle and up through my leg, coursing and throbbing from heel to hip.

Grandfather said, "The wound is clean and properly dressed. In time it should heal."

The sun was warm on my chest and face.

"Follow me, Grandson," he said.

With effort I could almost keep up with him. We went a short distance to the mesa's edge. Under the tower of rock where we stood looking down on Canyon del Muerto, the colors of the desert were muted, but each rabbit bush remained sharp and clean. The clear dazzling light had an autumn scent of cold juniper. The sour smell of bitterweed filtered through the sunlight and smelled both bitter and sweet.

Grandfather said, "Sit down, Grandson, on that rock there." He pointed to a stone that resembled a bench.

"Is this where you come to sit every morning?" I asked him.

He didn't answer me, but he smiled, and taking a pinch of cornmeal out of his deerskin medicine bag, he sprinkled it towards the sun. Then he scattered some golden white grains onto the earth, and finally, to the four directions. There was still a bit left in the bag, and this he put on his tongue, tasting it thoughtfully. Another pinch he put on top of my head and when I opened my mouth, he also placed a little on my tongue.

I knew this well—white cornmeal at morning, yellow at noon, black at night. Prayers to the Sun Father and Changing Woman, who is our Mother Earth. After being still for a while, Grandfather began to sing a song from *The Enemy Way*. I knew this, too, had heard it since I was very young. Soon he stopped, in midsong, and his voice trailed off.

"I sing to keep the ghosts off you," he explained.

"The ghosts?"

He then daubed the air all around me with an eagle feather.

"All ghosts," he answered vaguely, looking all about me, as if some of them lingered here, even in the bright morning light. Then he said, "You smell of death . . . you smell of murder and bullets and traitors. But, mostly, you smell of ghosts."

"From the fat man I killed?"

He dabbed at the air around my head and then passed the feather before my face several times. Then, holding it aloft, he whispered the chant of *All is Well*. He put the feather on the rock beside me.

"The earth has much death in it from long ago," he explained. He swallowed, breathed deeply, went on: "In the days when Monster Slayer, who is the son of the sun, killed all of the evil ones that went about the earth, there was death. From that time forward, the earth was red with the blood of those terrible dead things—giants. The song I sing is the one used long ago by Monster Slayer."

I nodded.

Far away there was a distant rumbling.

"Do you hear those far-off cannons?"

I tipped my head.

"They speak of death, too. The land is full of it. It's everywhere. So you see, the ghosts are wandering and dancing to this terrible music of cannon and murder and madness. They don't know where to go." He sighed, shut his eyes. He appeared to be listening to the cannons, but I knew that he was hearing something else. The earth, he was listening to the heartbeat of the earth. The dust drum of Changing Woman that drowned out the fire drum of the cannon's mouth.

Grandfather began singing again and he raised his voice with the words that send ghosts down into the underworld. Asking forgiveness of the "Ancient Ones," the people we call *Annuh Suzzie*, he sang blessings. These are the old ghosts that we have named Old Enemies because long ago we fought with them and beat them and took them as prisoners and slaves. Still, they taught us their medicine; and we've been ever thankful for that, which is why we ask their forgiveness for having killed them in the long ago. Well, they are gone now, but their ghosts are around to haunt us and, sometimes, to hurt us.

Grandfather got a sheep horn out of his bag. Using his fingernails, he scraped a ball of fat from the hollow part of the horn. The fat is sacred medicine; it comes from the mountain lion, the desert wolf, the river otter. He rolled the fat into a button, which he placed on the rock where I sat. Now he brushed the little button of grease with the black feather of a raven. He sang to it, as if it were alive, coaxing it to chase away the bad spirits.

Finally, he took up a third feather—this was a roadrunner's tail feather. Raising it to the sun, he continued his song while resting on his knees. After a little while, Grandfather stopped singing again and he started touching me on my hurt leg with the roadrunner's swiftness.

At last, he brought forth a folded piece of hide, opened it, and pinched its contents with thumb and forefinger. It was blue-gray ash and he put it on my bare leg, again and again.

"Do you know what this is?" he asked.

"Ash."

"Not just ash," he corrected. "This is from the burnt bones of the *Annuh Suzzie* killed by my great grandfather." I told him I knew of the story and he continued to pinch and sprinkle the bluish bone ash on each of my bare legs. Then he told me to be still, and he walked slowly back to the hogan. I closed my eyes and let the sun color my eyelids red.

When he returned he had my blood-dried moccasins in his hand.

They were full of sand.

"I put sand from a gopher hole into these," he explained, kneeling next to me. "They're no longer yours, these moccasins. They're going to stay here." He set them down near the cliff edge.

The two moccasins—one scarlet crusted, the other purple spotted—looked strange there, full of sand and ceremony, and decorated with my blood.

He said softly, "You must watch this now."

Raising his head toward the sun, he pinched—first his left nostril, then his right—as he inhaled sunlight. He did this four times, then told me to do the same thing, the same way. I did so.

"You have the sun within you now," he said. "The ghosts will be wary of approaching you."

Just then there came a great roar down in the canyon.

Rifles sputtered like so many pebbles hitting a wall.

"There are blue coats, pointing their long guns and firing up at us," Grandfather said. He seemed amused. "Brave men, shooting at an old man and a boy."

I stood up, leaned against my staff. The heavy blood pounded in my swollen leg.

Way down in the shadows wreathed in smoke haze, I saw a gathering of blue-coated soldiers.

Grandfather shook his head.

"In order to do one thing, they have to do other things that are worse. They wish to march us from our homeland. Therefore, they shoot and burn and pillage. Whatever's left of us, they gather up and march to Hweeldi."

I stared into the depths of the canyon. A band of Dineh were chained and strung out in a line, walking closely, heavily. Behind them, a wounded woman carrying a baby staggered and fell. A soldier reached out and took the baby away. I could hear the screams of mother and child all the way up on the mesa.

"Yes," I agreed. "It is their way."

We watched and the woman threw herself on the blue coat and pounded him with her fists. Pushing her aside—and holding her baby like a sack of grain—he took out his pistol and shot the woman. Then he tossed the baby on to the sand, and shot it, too.

The infant was ripped apart, torn like a blown leaf. The silent marching line of *Dineh* men moved quietly past the shadow of death, neither looking nor making any sign that they knew what was happening. They looked away; there was nothing else for them to do.

Then the wounded mother climbed shakily to her feet. Soaked in blood, she grasped a rock in her hands, and rushed at the soldier. Calmly, he fired at her from the hip. The woman, momentarily pinned to the wind, went back a step, wavered, and fell.

A dark Ute man rode up on a great black horse. I knew at once that this was the one we named Two Face.

"That one," Grandfather said, "has more hate in him than all the blue coats put together. He is the one responsible for all of this."

"He is worse than Kit Carson?"

I couldn't take my eyes off the tall, straight-backed, horse-riding Ute warrior. His face was painted in halves—blue and white. His scar ran from his forehead to his chin, marring the left side of his face, and making him look extremely ugly.

Trying to see him better, I squinted in the sunlight, shading my eyes with one hand.

"Does he really have yellow eyes, Grandfather?"

"Like *Maa'ii*, 'Old Man Coyote.'"

I knew Coyote could be a trickster—sometimes good, sometimes bad. Sometimes incredibly evil.

"He has much Coyote power," I commented. Unable to take my eyes off the dark man on his dark, dancing horse, I stared, as if in a trance.

"Better not look at him too hard," Grandfather warned. Pausing, he added, "Two Face knows who sees him."

We were both looking over the rim of the mesa. Two Face, riding elegantly, carried a buffalo tail whip.

"You see, Grandson, Two Face likes to show his superiority. He rides securely now, knowing that he has helped to round up so many of The People . . . but it will not always be so."

"What will happen?"

"Who can tell, Grandson?" He smiled bravely at the sun and said, "A man with so many names must be careful because someone will take them away from him, one by one. His names follow him like a ringed tail."

"What other names does he have?" I raised my leg behind me to keep the blood from rushing to my wound.

"Some people call him Red Shirt. Some call him Yellow because of his gold Coyote eyes. They are not really that color, but he can make it so, they tell me. Mostly, we call him Two Face. Although I prefer *Maa'ii,* Coyote, more than those other names since his coyote nature is the very thing that will one day prove to be his undoing."

I studied the man with the split face, who had so many names. I wished that I might be permitted to see the gold in his eyes when they changed to that color, but Grandfather told me we had to go back to the hogan.

"He seems so strong," I mentioned, as I hobbled.

"Any man bewitched by a bad coyote spirit can have such power. Yet, for the same reason, he can also lose it."

"How?"

"If we were to capture Two Face, and sing *The Coyote Bead Song* he would come to his senses."

I stopped shouldering myself along and leaned on my staff. My leg was beating like a drum; I raised it up behind me, away from the ground. Grandfather stopped walking. He gazed into my eyes briefly, then said, "If we use good medicine on him, he could be an ally, not an enemy. He could help us, then, to defeat the blue coats."

"But the Utes have always been our enemies. They're worse than the blue coats. That's what you've always said. Besides, anyone who is not *Dineh* must be *'eyoni,* an outsider. How could such a man help us?"

Grandfather smiled, "By not hurting us."

As we neared the doorway of the hogan, he told me, "A man is just a man. No more, no less. You must remember that. And even an evil man can change, can become good. Enemies are sometimes friends; friends are sometimes enemies."

He walked to where I stood resting like a heron, one-legged in the sun, and touched my arm with his hand.

"You cannot avoid seeing suffering, Grandson. But you must remember not to take pleasure in it. Nor should you ever enjoy the death of an enemy. There is no triumph in dying, or in killing. Least of all, in revenge. What we just witnessed, the suffering of our people in the Canyon del Muerto, shall pass before our eyes like the dew of death."

I thought about this for a long time as I lay down in the hogan, trying to blot out the picture of that woman and her baby. Worse, the image of Two Face . . . it haunted me now. I couldn't shake it. The truth was, I had really seen Two Face. And though I could not see his gold coyote eyes, I felt them.

I had seen him.

And I knew that he had seen me.

Wrinkled in the Wind

Three days after Grandfather did the second healing ceremony, Two Face rode away with four of his men and didn't return. More horsemen came into the canyon, the ones we call *Naakaii*, the Mexicans. Grandfather told me that they were no more to be trusted than the *Bilagaana*, the Americans.

On the fourth day Grandfather said, "We will move from this place. It's no longer safe."

That evening, we ate rock squirrel stew. There was nothing left to eat except prickly pear fruit. The squirrel meat was stringy. We also finished the last of our *Bilagaana* beans. I wondered where Grandfather was going to go. Was there any place left that was safe?

"Don't worry," he grinned when I asked him about it.

"I can't help worrying . . . I'll be a burden to you. I still cannot walk without the staff."

"We have strong medicine," he said confidently. "Nothing can harm us."

"Where does your medicine come from, Grandfather?"

I was eating the last of our stew, rubbing my fingers around the gourd bowl, and sucking them clean. Crouched in front of juniper coals, I waited for his answer. Somewhere in the deep night, a nighthawk dived and roared, open-mouthed as it fell from a great height, catching insects on the wing. A little canyon owl whimpered in the shivering starlight. I dipped my first three fingers into the stew pot, and wiped the bottom dry. As I licked the last of the stew gravy, I glanced into Grandfather's eyes. Though encased in wrinkles, his old eyes glittered like the fire coals that warmed us. With his red headband and his flowing white hair, he was still a worthy warrior.

"All this happened a long time ago," he said slowly, and I knew that he was about to answer my question with a story. "It happened when the months of middle summer come together. It happened on the mesa top known as Earth Whirling. Do you know where it is?"

I said that I did.

Remembering, his eyes misted and he reached back into the time of beginnings. Our beginnings, The People's.

Then he told the story of Elder Brother, the one known as Nayenezgani, twin brother of Tobachischin, my namesake. Elder Brother, as Nayenezgani is known, had angered White Thunder. And White Thunder revenged himself by shattering Elder Brother with a bolt of lightning. Off Earth Whirling he went, falling down into the desert.

"Why did White Thunder do this thing?" I asked. Grandfather rolled a corn leaf cigarette, sprinkled some black tobacco into it, and lit it with a juniper twig. He drew the harsh smoke into his lungs and let it out a little bit at a time. The smoke smelled good in the evening air.

"Elder Brother was too far from his place; from where the gods had told him to be. He knew that, but he was always a bold one, making decisions on his own. So he'd trod on the sacred ground of the gods, and after this he was punished. Disobedient, he learned things the hard way."

Grandfather flicked his cigarette ash into the fire. Then he drew in the smoke and again blew it into the hogan. It hung briefly, as if undecided, before the smoke hole banished it into the cool night air.

I understood that Nayenezgani was punished for being out of place. This made me think of my parents—they, too, had stayed in Canyon del Muerto, even after our chiefs had said to go, to scatter to the winds. We stayed on when we should've gone. Other *Dineh* were on the move, going west towards the Lukachukai, because the blue coats, the Utes, and the *Naakaii* were also on the move, hunting them. They were always after us. But, our family stayed. Father had said no one would trouble us.

Where was our place? I wondered. Where were we supposed to be? Did Grandfather know?

"From that," Grandfather went on, "Elder Brother learned where he was supposed to go, and where he was not supposed to go. It was a valuable lesson." He tapped his corn husk cigarette and drew on it again so that the end of the husk flared and dimmed. The bittersweet smoke circled me with a blue snake-like wreath that unraveled and disappeared.

"Is that what we must learn, Grandfather . . . our place? Will all this be over when we find our proper place?"

His eyes glittered wisely; he flicked his cigarette into the fire. Grandfather was old like the land, like the earth itself but his spirit was never tired, always renewing itself. And, like the arroyos, he had weathered many storms and knew his own high-water mark.

"We," he whispered, almost chanting, "are like our cousin, Wolf. The one we call *Maiit'so*, 'Big Wanderer.' He's always moving, that one is. Going and coming. That's his way—his place. Our way's to move, too. That's our place, or at least it was. Now it seems to be different. Now it seems the times are changed, ever changing. Now we must settle—somewhere else. We must find a new place. A new *Dineh* ground that is holy."

He sighed and in the round afterglow of the fire coals, his eyes kept their starry twinkle. After a long silence, he settled down on his blanket by the fire.

"You asked about my medicine," he chuckled before he went to sleep. "Where does it come from? Well, it comes . . . "

In the darkness came the whimper of an owl.

We listened.

Then he said so softly I could barely hear him, "It comes from . . . remembering."

I thought about this for quite a while, and long after Grandfather had gone to sleep, I was still thinking. I remembered the story of Big Wanderer, how he went away during the Great Flood. First Man told him to find the source of the dawn, but he went away. And has been away ever since. Coyote came and stole the stars, and has stolen valuable things ever since. I, too, remembered.

In the beginning, we, The People, lived under the earth, in darkness. We came out, into the light. But, now, where were we supposed to go? And what had we done to be punished so? Were we like Elder Brother? Had we trespassed on sacred ground?

These thoughts turned in my mind as the stars wheeled overhead. I slept, fitfully, taking care not to roll on my injured leg.

I was glad of Grandfather's medicine.

Glad of remembering, glad of being alive.

That night I dreamed of water, wrinkled in the wind.

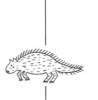

A Shadow of Shadows

The next morning, the fifth day after my injury, Grandfather made a small bowl of cornmeal mush. We ate out of two gourds of the wild squash. Pinching the wet cornmeal with forefinger and thumb, we swallowed in silence. The mush was warm and good and the little grains stuck to my teeth, and worked their way through them. After the meal, Grandfather told me to follow him out into the sun.

He walked quickly and I limped along, moving better than the day before. I used the staff less and I could put my full weight down on my right foot.

"I had a dream last night," he said. "I dreamed of horses. They were having their teeth pulled. Have you ever had this dream?"

I laughed, said no.

"This is a warning dream," he said seriously.

"What does it mean?"

He surveyed the flat table of rock, the mesa that was his home. The ochre and rust-colored rock stretched like a blanket woven of the earth's prettiest wool. Here were seams, there were threads. Here the wool was raveled, there unraveled.

"Today a messenger will come," Grandfather said.

He scanned the landscape, looking for I knew not what.

He said no more and I knew that I couldn't ask him what he meant about the messenger; yet if I waited, an answer would, sooner or later, come of its own accord. I was full of questions like a pot that boils over, but I had no choice other than to wait patiently.

We walked to a clear pool of rainwater that hadn't dried up. Deep and unruffled, it was the color of pine sap. The wind played on it and the pool shivered and Grandfather filled two bags made from the stomach skin of the mountain sheep.

"We'll need this water on our way," he explained. Then he beckoned to me and I walked towards the mesa's edge where he'd gone, and we stared across the purple and mauve desert morning, and I suddenly remembered last night's dream of water. And here it was—heavy in the sheepskins, water!

Was that the strong medicine of remembering? Did I have the power within me, too?

Down in the canyon we heard the heavy-wheeled, mule-pulled carts of the *Naakaii*. The sound of their whips cracking was an insult to the air. The horsemen had hairy faces and they wore sleeveless shirts of rawhide. They were dressed for war. *Naakaii* is a bitter word.

"We're surrounded, you see," Grandfather mumbled, kneeling on one knee. Cradling his chin in his hand, he stared thoughtfully down into the canyon shadows of moving men, horses, carts, mules, whips, and the rising dust that they stirred in their wake. I felt my belly growl, but the noise was covered up by these other sounds.

"How are we going to get away then?"

"The same way that the messenger will come see us."

"How is that?"

"Secretly."

I wasn't sure what he was talking about, but some moments later Grandfather took me to a tiny cave between two huge boulders of lichen-covered rock. In the darkness of the cave something was darkly gesturing—I could feel it more than see it. A jiggling, a flickering. Then, nothing. Grandfather felt the thing himself, for I saw him take a prayer stick from his bag.

The prayer stick was painted black and it was decorated with red and white lightning.

Tenderly, as if the stick were alive, he placed it at the mouth of the cave, and I watched as he put it there and I saw a trembling in the cave, a shadow that lived in shadow.

Then, while we watched, that great, ugly lizard known as Gila Monster came out into the front of the cave so that the light of day touched his blotchy scarlet and black skin.

I saw him clearly, the red and black splotches on his beaded face. Old Man Gila Monster, the ugly one.

Grandfather chanted high in his throat, "Old Man, give us your blessing." He chanted of the missing parts that come together; his voice was sharp like striking flint. Then the Old Man in the cave got up a little, his left hand wiggling like a piece of greasewood in the wind.

The chant asked the lizard guardian for the black shield of flint, the warrior armor that protects travelers.

This was the song of asking and if Old Man Gila Monster wanted to grant this thing, we would see it, we would know it.

Grandfather went on singing and his words were hanging on the wind and the lizard watched us from the folds of his deeply buried, old man's furrowed eyes.

Down below the cart people cursed, cracked their whips, and the dust billowed up and spread out like rose-colored flour.

In the cave Old Man Gila Monster raised his left hand higher and he pointed it at us; and it trembled like he was having a fit. For a long time, we sat motionless, watching. Then the chant ended and the ancient lizard put down his hand. The blessing was finished.

Grandfather looked exhausted. Beads of sweat stood out on his upper lip where his thin, wispy mustache was. "He has given us his power," Grandfather said tiredly. "Now we must await the messenger."

Suddenly—I don't know how—I, too, felt the coming of the messenger—who, or whatever, it was. Yes, as surely as the clouds swallowed the sun and darkened the day, I felt the coming of someone, some thing, something.

And, yet, by the middle of that day my leg had stopped hurting altogether and I had stopped limping. There was nothing left of the injury except the long irregular scar, and the strange vibration of the toes of my left foot. All that day I wondered how we were to live without food, Grandfather and me, isolated and trapped on our bare rock above the endless desert sand. How could a shadow of shadows save us?

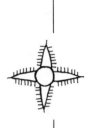

Our Eyes Are Sharp as Flint

My toes tingled as I fell asleep that night, hungry for the first time. We had nothing to eat. Still, I was not afraid. Had I not seen the trembling hand of Old Man Gila Monster? Had I not seen it with my own eyes, as it wiggled the same way that a medicine man's hand quivers over the body of a sick person? Old Man Gila Monster, Grandfather said before he slept, was the secret of our well-being. But—how? I knew, I believed that I knew, but I didn't know how, or why. I had faith . . . or did I? Why was I so uncertain if I wasn't afraid?

I wanted to believe, to fully believe, that was all. Old Man Gila Monster was my ally, as well as Grandfather's. His power was our power. But my mind raced over other things and took me to places I didn't want to go.

I thought of Two Face. His ally was Coyote—a tricky, strong, unpredictable warrior. We had no way of knowing how, or where, he might strike. Was our power—Gila Monster's—stronger than Coyote's? I couldn't remember a story that pitted these two legendary people against one other. Coyote, I knew, had rain and storm at his beckoning. Gila Monster had flint and lightning. Each one had fire.

In this way, my mind went spinning and I wasn't able to get any sleep.

When, at last, I dropped off, I had a dream—or what I think was a dream. Anyway, I woke abruptly and the hogan was bright white, as if a star were burning inside of it. Out of the corona of brightness came a tall man, wearing a white deerskin shirt. He had well-groomed hair, long and black, and it fell thickly upon his shoulders and over his back. He wore a red breechcloth and fine moccasins with intricate beadwork on them.

The tall man's smile was gracious and warm, and there was goodwill in it, as there was goodness in his presence, and the light all about him shone magnificently. When the tall man smiled, his teeth were like white corn, gleaming and straight. He bore no weapon, not even a knife. He stood, open-handed, smiling at me. Then, as quickly as he'd appeared, he vanished. The starlight was gone; the hogan was dark.

And now I woke up again, realizing that it had all been a dream, that the man was not real, he was a phantom. The hogan was still except for the breathing of Grandfather and the chirping of the crickets. I rubbed my eyes, looked around. The night held its breath.

A dream? Yet it seemed so true, so brightly true. What a strange dream. I couldn't forget it, nor could I sleep. I would doze, then come awake, thinking the tall man was there. Somewhere in the heart of the ticking canyon, a coyote yipped. Then, the sad sound of some musical instrument, accompanied by a man's voice. A

Naakaii, singing in Spanish. Somehow the unfamiliar floating words, borne on the wind, reminded me of my dead parents and their journey through the underworld and I knew that I, too, would be making that journey, and then I couldn't stop my body from shaking.

When I next opened my eyes, Grandfather was baking a seed cake in the hot ash of the morning's fire.

"How are you, Grandson?" he asked as he cut the seed cake into two pieces, handing one to me.

"I hardly feel any pain in my leg," I told him.

"It is good."

He broke apart a small bit of his cake and offered it to the fire, a custom I knew well. For it is the spirit of the fire that is one of our oldest ancestors. The dull ache in my ankle reminded me that something had happened there, but that was all. There was no more shooting, climbing pain. Nor was there any numbness. I had my leg; this day I would walk like a man.

"Where did you get this cake?"

"I made it."

"From what?"

He gave me a curious glance. Smiling, he said, "Old Man Gila Monster pointed west; I went in that direction and found little blooming plants with hard, good seeds."

"What are they?"

"Ground squirrel's winter feast . . . may he forgive us."

Grandfather nibbled his seed cake. He plucked at his mustache, said, "The time will come soon when you will need to run on that leg. Thanks to Old Man Gila Monster, you will do so."

In my heart I thanked the ugly old lizard . . . for he was ugly and old, as well as beneficial. I remembered his gnarled face of darkish blood, his body of armored flint, his fatness—his bloated hands and feet.

In my heart I thanked him, even though he was so ugly.

I nibbled my seed cake so that it would last longer.

"Is Old Man Gila Monster a witch?" I asked.

Grandfather laughed, plucked his mustache hairs again.

Then he blew the ash off his cake. "He has the will to do good or evil. It is in him, just as it is in us, to perform deeds that are fine and acts that are wicked. We should be careful, Grandson, what we ask of him—or anyone who has great stores of power."

I asked if he thought Old Man Gila Monster was stronger than Old Man Coyote, for this was the thing that was bothering me. At this, he laughed until he shook. His wrinkled face was leather-marked.

"They are both of equal strength," he said with a grin, giving me a sidelong look with his laughing eyes.

I thought about this and then he said that we'd had a visitor that night.

"Last night?"

"Yes."

"A tall, handsome-faced, well-clothed man?"

"Just as you say."

"Was he bright like a star?"

"He was that way."

I asked more questions and Grandfather said he'd baked the man a seed cake. I saw it lying there in the sand at the front of the doorway where the morning sun was touching it. The cake was centered in the moccasin print, the single moccasin print of the tall man. There were no other prints, anywhere near there, just that one—and in it, the little cake. It lay in the morning sun with the blue ash still on it. I looked at the print while I savored my own cake. The weight of the foot that made the deep track there by the door was proof of a large, tall person. Someone much taller than Grandfather.

At last Grandfather told me, "The one who made that track was sent by a sorcerer. It happened while we were sleeping."

I remembered my dream perfectly. Again, I pictured the handsome, well-groomed man, and the shining that came off him and filled the hogan with a star's coldness and brightness.

"Did the man have only one leg?" I questioned.

"The man who came was a spirit sent by another man. He, the one who visited us, left a single track to show us that we are weak—me, an old man, you a mere boy with an injured leg. This is the sign of a sorcerer's power and his knowledge of us."

Then he added firmly, "Do not look at that track any longer, Grandson. You'll give it more strength."

"We could use that seed cake," I suggested.

"No," he said scolding. "I left that there to tell the sorcerer that we eat well—so well that we can feed a spirit that needs no earth food."

He finished his cake and wiped his mouth.

Sometime after, when the sun was at midpoint, he brushed the track clean with a cedar brush, but by then the cake was missing, gone. I never knew, nor cared, where it went, or who took it. It was not for us, that was all.

Walking around on the mesa, I felt so good I could walk without my staff. The soreness in the bone lingered a little longer, but the sharp pain was not there anymore when I stepped down and put my full weight on my foot. Given time, I'd be able to run. I wondered how soon that might be; how soon I'd have to try.

Grandfather told me that in just a little while we would go off the mesa, but he wouldn't say exactly when. Although we were surrounded by *Naakaii* and Ute, too, he nonetheless had a plan. But what it was I couldn't imagine. So I spent the rest of the day wondering. Down in the canyon the sun pounded the red rock walls, dispelling the shadows, and then as it went higher, letting them return. I went to Old Man Gila Monster's cave, but there was no one there. I waited in the late cicada-singing afternoon, but no one came out of the dark. Perhaps it would only happen with Grandfather's song.

I watched the clouds as they grew large and lifted over us, going west, always going west. Like the white canvas wagons of the *Bilagaana*, I saw them roll by, the clouds, wishing one might stop and take me along. I would ride that cloud away, far away.

Down on a shelf of canyon rock, I spotted a huge yucca plant, the kind we call *yay bi tsa si*. From where I sat on my lookout, I saw the sharp-tipped leaves of the spiked plant; it lived on a little ledge all by itself. The fruit it bore was fat and ripe, and ready for picking—if I could somehow get hold of it. I went back to the hogan and got Grandfather's horsehair rope. Back at the lookout, I built a loop, and after several tries, I captured the yucca and dislodged it. My mouth watered when I saw the huge bulbs of good roasting fruit, and I proudly brought three of them to Grandfather. "Tonight," he grinned, "we'll feast. I've got enough cornmeal to make one small corn cake and we'll roast the *yay bi tsa si*." But as he said this, my stomach heard, and growled. Grandfather smiled and told me, "Our stomachs need to be still when visitors come." I wondered what he meant by visitors and he cautioned, "When visitors come our eyes should be sharp as flint."

Uninvited by the Fire

We did feast that night and Grandfather built up the fire and put a big juniper knot onto the coals. Such a knot would burn all night. Then he rolled up in his blanket and was fast asleep. I slept too because my belly had something in it, finally, and I felt at peace.

However, a short time after I fell asleep I woke up. A small hunchback man was in the doorway of the hogan. He looked very poor with his flimsy shirt of wood rat skins and his sandals made of woven grass, and his sad old bow and puny arrows. By the look of him, a man without a tribe, without any place to go. Was this the visitor Grandfather had expected?

"Greetings to each of you," the thin man said, smiling crookedly. He lay down his bow by the door. Then he took off his rabbit fur quiver, and set it aside on the sand beside the bow.

Grandfather was sitting up, poking at the fire. He acted as if this stranger came visiting all the time. Meanwhile, the thin man leaned wearily in the doorway. Over his shoulder, toward the east rim of the mesa, the stars still blazed. Grandfather stirred the fire and the thin man said, "Where are all the men of your camp?"

"They have gone off hunting," Grandfather snorted. He didn't look up; he kept poking the embers, and the juniper smoke sweetened the hogan as it rose on the wobbly air and mingled with the stars.

The thin man shifted from foot to foot. "Have you come a long way?" Grandfather asked him, glancing at him for the first time.

The bony stranger nodded.

"Well," Grandfather yawned, "Do you want a blanket to sit on?"

The stranger was eager to have one, so I dusted off a sheepskin, which was all that we had, and the scrawny fellow folded his legs on top of it, and leaned nearer to the fire. Then he raised his open palms to the curling flames, and sighed with satisfaction.

"You see that I am poor," he said, apologetically. He looked at me rather than Grandfather as he spoke. "Like you, I belong to the earth," he said in his quiet voice of sadness. "But, unlike you, I own nothing except the worn fur that I wear."

While the man talked, Grandfather glanced at him, neither interested nor amused, I thought. He seemed— as I was—to be considering whether the stranger were a liar, or a mystery-man like the earlier dream visitor we'd had. I decided to believe him, the thin man, but Grandfather said, "I've heard that those of the earth, people like you, always keep good tobacco on them." His voice was sharp, his tone full of sarcasm.

The stranger grinned and looked sheepishly at us. Then he reached for a pouch that hung from his belt. The pouch was covered with painted suns and moons. The design of these was much faded, yet you could see that it was once a fine possession. Inside it there was a pipe of clay, some tobacco, and a few other herbs as well. The stranger packed the pipe with his dark brown tobacco, tamped it well with his thumb, and then placed it by the fire.

Grandfather nodded for him to light it, and he did, using a fire stick. When the pipe was drawing nicely, the thin man blew smoke into the four directions, then he offered the pipe to Grandfather, who did the same thing.

After a while, Grandfather cradled the pipe in his arms showing, perhaps, that he was in no hurry to be done with it. Presently, he put it to his lips again and drew deeply on it and the fragrant smoke filled the hogan. The blue plumes reluctantly snaked upwards, where they were sucked out of the smoke hole.

I don't know why—maybe it was Old Man Gila Monster's wisdom—but it came to me that the stranger's tobacco was not good. Though it smelled nice, it might be bad medicine. I eyed Grandfather and he seemed calm, yet his forehead was wet with sweat, staining his bandanna. His hands, too, were starting to shake and his eyelids drooped and fluttered.

At this, the stranger smiled. He appeared most pleased and I had the urge to reach for the long knife Grandfather kept behind the buffalo skull. However, as I watched and my heart quickened, a magic thing happened. *Niltsi,* the wind, came up and danced playfully around the eight-sides of the hogan. A sign, I thought, *Niltsi* is looking after us. And as *Niltsi* danced outside, the stranger quickly lost his crooked smile.

At the same time, Grandfather's eyes opened wide and the sweat dried on his damp face and now it was his turn to grin. The stranger's silence became awkward, uneasy. And I knew that that tobacco would've killed a lesser man than Grandfather.

Grandfather, of course, knew it as well. However, he was content to keep quiet about it, to play along with the stranger's game. Outside, *Niltsi* danced louder all round the hogan, stirring up puffs of dust. Finally, Grandfather handed the stranger's pipe back to him. "Nephew," he said politely in his soft-as-ash voice, "I like your smoke but there is one thing I need to ask you."

The thin man shrugged, a half-smile on his narrow lips. "I have no secrets," he said, trying to sound easy and indifferent.

Grandfather grinned at him, said, "When may I have some more?"

Our guest chuckled nervously. Knocking the burnt tobacco into the fire, he dipped the pipe, tamped it, and passed it back to Grandfather, who lit it as before with a tapered firebrand. I looked at the thin man. His face in the firelight was a mask of forced friendliness.

With a brittle formality, he extended the pipe to Grandfather, who took it up, saying, "All right, Nephew, may I put a bit of my own blend into this?"

I think I saw the stranger flinch when he said this. But he answered, "Do what you will, I am your guest."

"Then the honor of your visit must be returned." He paused, and added subtly, "in equal measure, Nephew." Grandfather then reached for a pouch that was tied to the right horn of the buffalo skull. Undoing the drawstring, he dipped the clay pipe inside and filled it a third time. When the pipe was fully tamped, Grandfather offered it to the thin man.

"As our guest you shall have the first taste."

The stranger nodded, his urgent eyes glittering nervously. *Niltsi*, at the doorway, tickled up some dust as the thin man drew on the pipe, and made his gestures to the directions. No sooner had he done so than *Niltsi* rushed down the smoke hole, and punched the fire with a gust of cold air that sent juniper smoke into the thin man's face. Coughing, he dropped the pipe.

When he looked up again, his eyes were full of smoke-tears. He rubbed them and continued to cough. Then, he gave us a sudden, startled stare and the life seemed to leave him, and he laid his chin on his breastbone like a dead bird and crumpled on to the sheepskin, sound asleep.

Chuckling, Grandfather said, "He will be like that for some time. Maybe, when he wakes, he'll try another foolish trick that his teacher taught him."

"Who is his teacher?" I asked.

"The same one who sent us that other messenger."

"Two Face?"

"He is the only one I know who can work such magic."

I was amazed at how well and how quickly Grandfather had settled this thing, and I said, "Look how he sleeps, uninvited, by the fire."

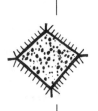

Arrow Through the Heart

I dozed off for a while after that and then at first light I woke to the smell of rabbit stew. How Grandfather had snared a rabbit, I will never know. For there aren't any rabbits on the mesa. The thin man was outside, by then, stretching in the sunlight. In the clear light of day, he was smaller and shabbier than the night before. How had he gotten up the walls of Canyon del Muerto to our hogan—was he a spider person? Did he have wings? He looked ordinary, very ordinary—and he was no dream phantom, I knew that. This man was flesh-and-bone, commanded in some way by a power as great as Grandfather's. And I wondered, what would he try to do now?

Grandfather had baked flat bread on the hot stones of the fire pit. This was made from the soft white, powdery flour of the *Naakaii*. My mouth watered when I saw those *Naakaii* things called tortillas. There was a brown stew bubbling in an old black battered pot.

I watched Grandfather as he prepared the morning meal, putting the flat bread into one of our poison baskets. This was a thing that only our clan knew about, no one else. At the point where the coil of the basket ends, the poison begins; that's the way it is done. A chill crept into my bones when I saw the basket laid out so; and when the thin man sat down cross-legged and gave me a heavy-lidded look, I knew that another contest was about to start. I stared hungrily at the tortillas, wishing they were all mine and that this game of life and death was done.

Grandfather offered our guest the flat bread in the basket. He put it in the stranger's hands, with the finished coil, facing out, toward the man. As he passed the tortillas, Grandfather shared a knowing glance with me, but of course I made no sign that I saw it.

The stranger accepted the food, nodding gratefully, completely unaware. His eyes shifted about the basket, though, as if he were looking for something he could not see. He stared at the small round inviting breads, then he said, "Where I come from, we always eat from the place opposite the last coil on the basket."

Grandfather said, "You do? Nephew, that is strange." Grandfather's use of the polite word, nephew, was sarcasm, but the thin man never seemed to notice.

Now he selected a tortilla from our side of the basket, well away from the coil of poison. He munched it down with a smile.

Grandfather grinned, "You eat from the wrong place, Nephew."

The thin man, munching contentedly, paid him no mind. He ate the tortilla, licked his lips and then his fingertips. "Hmm," he mumbled, pleased, as he gave the stew pot a glance with his sleepy-seeming eyes.

In spite of the poison basket, my belly grumbled. I

wondered if the stew had some secret in it, too—something to be overcome. I wanted this thing to be over—this undeclared battle of mystery-man magic. But in spite of it all, I began to eat the tortillas, making sure mine were well away from the little death's head coil.

Then Grandfather offered the thin man a second basket, a smaller one, in which there was a single corn cake.

"Our custom," Grandfather remarked, "is to give a small portion of what we eat to Old Man Fire. Do you not do the same?"

He pinched off a piece of leftover tortilla and gently placed it on top of the fire coals where it smoked and shriveled into a frail little cinder.

The thin man followed this with a tortilla piece of his own, but he eyed the corn cake greedily while Grandfather set bowls of steaming rabbit stew before us.

The basket with the golden corn cake looked innocent, but the thin man wasn't sure what to do. He wanted the cake—yet he was not about to take it. Instead he stared at it longingly, suspiciously.

Grandfather said, "Our way is to eat from around the edge of the cake."

The thin man's eyes darted and his crooked smile returned.

"Where I come from," he suggested, "we eat only from the middle." Smiling, his uneven front teeth came over his bottom lip so that he looked like a rabbit.

"Very well, do it your way," Grandfather agreed, as the thin man plunged his dirty fingers into the center of the corn cake. When he brought it to his mouth, the golden crumbs tumbled down his chest.

"Good," Grandfather said approvingly. "I can see that you like it."

The stranger stopped chewing. He stared stonily at us. I ignored him, however, as I used my first three fingers to scoop up the savory rabbit stew. The corn cake, glowing like a small sun, was between us, untouched but for the torn out portion the thin man had eaten.

He seemed to stop chewing. He looked out of glazed eyes as we ate. Then I heard him snoring, whistling through his nose. The little man was asleep with his head down like a bird with its face on its breast.

As we ate, the thin man snored and Grandfather chuckled.

"Help me get him to his feet," Grandfather said, when we'd finished our meal.

I did that thing, taking hold of the thin man's wrists as Grandfather got his feet, and we carried him out of the hogan.

"Where are we going?" I asked.

"We're going to throw him off the cliff."

"Grandfather—do you mean it?"

He chuckled, then grinned. "He lost." More chuckling, grinning.

Even with my sore leg, I was able to lift and hold the thin man. He weighed, it seemed, less than an owl child.

When we got to the slab of sunlit stone that was the cliff edge, Grandfather asked, "Is this where you first laid eyes on Two Face?"

"Yes," I told him.

Down on the desert floor, a couple of magpies were chasing after one another, crying *poot*, *poot*, and sailing comically through the shadow-land of the desert. A blue-tail lizard scampered nervously at my feet. I felt the sun hot on my neck. The rising air, though, was juniper cool, still fresh from the night's dew.

Just then, as we were about to drop him, the thin

man came to his senses. Yellow corn cake spittle ran from his grayish chin.

"What . . . have . . . you done?" he stammered. He cocked his head from side to side, amazed at where he was, and how we were holding him, and what we were about to do to him.

"We're tossing you off the cliff, Nephew," Grandfather told him in a mocking voice.

"—Why?" the thin man asked. He was straining to free himself but we held him fast.

"It is our custom to throw away that which we have no use for," Grandfather said.

Then he nodded at the cliff edge and said, to me, "All right, Grandson."

A light throw, and the stranger sent up to kill us by Two Face was rolling through the dry desert air, spinning like a pine cone. We watched him as he dropped; he made no sound. But when he struck the earth in a fountain of dust, he let out a bursting noise.

I thought he would explode like a great bag of blood.

Instead he went off like a dust devil. We followed him with our eyes as he wheeled away, wobbling and crazy, until the distance devoured him.

"Two Face won't waste himself with more assassins," Grandfather told me as we walked back to the hogan. "His next visit will be an arrow through the heart."

Forefoot of the Lizard

The threat of capture was warded off by Grandfather's magic, but I knew that our time on the mesa was finished. We needed to find another sanctuary—but where?

Two Face was close by, waiting. And for him the taking of prisoners was a kind of game. To win, sometimes, it was necessary to lose, as he had with Grandfather. But that was how he measured his foes, testing their power and permitting them, perhaps, to beat him as he sought the source of their strength.

Now that he knew Grandfather was a man of power, what, I wondered, would he try next?

That night the autumn moon filled the canyon, which echoed with *Naakaii* foot soldiers. Some of them posing as allies of the Americans captured *Dineh* to sell as slaves. Our people were then taken to the silver mines of Cerrillos and the haciendas of Lamy. All this we knew because it had happened before and would happen again. I asked myself if it would ever end . . . if there would ever be peace.

The Utes, our oldest of enemies, didn't want to take us alive. The blue coats paid the same price for scalps as for men. And scalps were easier to carry and there was no need to feed them.

The morning after the harvest moon I saw a Ute bounty hunter, his bridle strung with scalp locks. He rode into the canyon; I watched him from above. The *Naakaii* drove mule trains that hauled long, feather-limbed spruce trees. These were stripped and carved into crude ladders designed for scaling the mesa. In a few days, the *Naakaii* would be at our doorway. I asked Grandfather where we were going to go. He was outside the hogan, sitting cross-legged in the sun smoking a cigarette.

"There's a secret canyon like this one on the west of Lukachukai. I've heard about it. There are plenty of *maroons* there as the *Naakaii* call them—you know, *Dineh* who refuse to give up the old way, hunting and living off the land." He drew deeply on his cigarette and blew a stream of smoke into the pale sunlight. "The secret place is called *Tseyaa deez'ahi*; you've heard me speak of it, Grandson."

"Will we go to it by day, or by night?"

"Both, Grandson."

Shortly after this, he packed our things for the long journey. There was little to carry—two sheepskins, one water pouch. I had the obsidian knife that was given to me by my father and an extra pair of moccasins given to me by my mother. Grandfather gave me one other thing before we started out that day.

"I want you to have this," he said solemnly.

Handing me a cowry shell a little larger than my thumbnail, he said, "Put this under your tongue and it will stop your thirst."

I did as he said and the little shell felt cool and clean, and the little bumps where it folded were pleasant to my tongue. Soon my mouth was full of water. Amazed, I swallowed. "It works," I told him. He grinned as he rolled his sheepskin and tied it with a deer-hide lace, then he told me, "White Shell Woman is the bringer of rain and water, as you know. This tiny shell is her gift to The People. I've had it as long as I can remember and it has always served me well. Do you know the story of it?"

I shook my head.

"They say the first people were once lost in the desert and couldn't find their way. They had no water, so Coyote dug into the ground. He made a clay jar and he put a shell like this one into it. The jar filled with water." I said, "Coyote did good things back then. Why doesn't he do them now?"

Grandfather slung the rolled sheepskin over his shoulder as he replied, "He will work for us again—you will see." Then for the last time he went into our hogan. I stood in the doorway and watched him strike flint to steel. He was going to build a fire. What a strange thing to do, I thought, just as we're about to leave. He came out into the yellow sunlight, a gust of smoke following him. Then I understood what he was doing: He was burning the hogan so no ghosts, or *chindi*, would follow us on our journey.

"This smoke will draw the *Naakaii*," he said, waving the thick smoke away from his face. "They will work fast to get their ladders up. In their haste, they'll make mistakes. When they try to scale the wall, some will fall and be hurt."

He smiled, stroked his chin. "We'll know nothing of this," he said, tugging the white mustache hairs at the side of his mouth. "We'll be like this smoke carried by the wind, far away from here."

Then we started out, walking towards the east side of the mesa. Grandfather had a walking stick. Bent and blackened with age, it seemed a foolish thing to take along with us. It was too short to put weight upon, too long to stow in one's belt.

"If anything happens to me, Tobachischin," he said, "you'll have two medicine allies to help you."

I could only think of one: the cowry shell. Then he held up the ancient, fire-blackened walking stick. "This looks like a useless stick of greasewood, but it can do things. You'll see."

Behind us the hogan was ablaze, showering the turquoise sky with angry sparks that buzzed like red bees. The cedar log rafters belched tongues of flame. The roof groaned, started to sag and fall down at one end. I looked to the east away from the fire and we walked on to the edge of the mesa.

Grandfather stuck the walking stick out towards the sun and it tipped downward, pointing into the shadow-lands of the canyon.

"It points down, does it not?"

I nodded. "It bends hard towards the earth."

Grandfather tugged his mustache. Black smoke, pitch smoke, hovered over our heads. Two ravens chopped by and I heard the *whump, whump* of their wing-strokes. The noon sun stung the back of my neck, but my mouth—thanks to the shell—was wet. I remembered Grandfather saying to me once, "Sun Father sometimes burns us, yet Changing Woman, Mother Earth, always shields His heat."

Suddenly the walking stick, which grandfather was still holding began to shake. Then it drew a line on the red rimrock.

The stick vibrated like the forefoot of the lizard.

Night Cry of a Coyote

Grandfather stayed a long time, holding the stick and feeling its vibrations. The black smoke passed over us like Great Snake, coiling and curving away and up over the mesa. I looked down into the canyon where the silver-blue sage dotted the long, low-lying shadow country. Little scarves of dust came twirling up canyon on the wind and the great puffy clouds shed dark blossoms on the land as they passed overhead.

Suddenly I heard a chattering noise and there was a ground squirrel sitting atop a rock, not five hands away from Grandfather. The ground squirrel was talking and Grandfather was nodding, as if he understood exactly what this animal person was saying.

"He's telling us how to get off the mesa without being seen," Grandfather said to me. The ground squirrel had thirteen lines, or stripes, on his back. I wondered what they meant, then remembered what Grandfather once told me. "Those lines are for the thirteen months of our year, the Navajo year. The thirteenth month is called Coyote Moon and it is a time when the mystery of winter is deepening. This is a time when no one knows what will happen—Coyote's tricks are his own secret."

But now Grandfather pointed towards the ground squirrel and said, "Look, he is showing the way."

"Won't your walking stick tell us?"

"That stick only knows the *direction*, not the way."

Grandfather moved nimbly along the rimrock while in front of him, running in zigzags, went the squirrel. I felt my leg start to ache as I tried to run on it; our journey was already hard on the newly mended bone, but I kept up just the same.

As we trotted along the mesa's rim, I told Grandfather that I knew why the squirrel's stripes were set that way, and I told him what I remembered. He replied, "You remember well, Grandson. The thirteenth month is that time when Coyote stole the stars from First Man, who told him to put them back. The thirteenth month is also when he, Coyote, put them back in their original place." Then the ground squirrel stopped and peered into a thicket of gold-flowered snakeweed. Nervously, he darted into a hole concealed by the brilliant bush.

"This is where we must go," said Grandfather, pointing into the hole, then getting down on his knees and peering into it. A red-shouldered hawk floated over, his shadow rippling on the hot brown rock.

I looked into the tiny hole where the ground squirrel had gone. Grandfather put out his walking stick; it pointed down as before, quivering at the squirrel hole.

"This the place," Grandfather confirmed, "Let us follow our cousin."

Then he began blowing softly into the little dark cavity. Four breaths, then four more. Another four, another four. The rhythm of his breathing—*whuff, whuff, whuff, whuff*—was the patient, cleaving beat of a drum. As he expelled with his lungs, the afternoon went overhead on the wings of a red-shouldered hawk. Distance grew closer, farther came nearer. Shadows veiled and unveiled; time ticked in the heart of a cricket. The sun drew behind an immense wintry-coated cloud, washing the mesa blue and cold. The companion hawk cried out his high, thin wailing sun chant.

Grandfather, who was lying on his side staring into the hole, grinned at me. "It is good," he said, and I knew he meant the moment. Then, as I looked on that tiny crack in the earth, it widened, opened. The earth spilled into it, as if something drew it down. There was a growling noise in the belly of the big stone mesa, and a little grumbling, and then all was still. The hawk's shadow stole away, sweeping time with it, erasing our tracks, our presence. The hole of the ground squirrel yawned open—grown great in size, turned into a tunnel. And it beckoned us to follow.

"You go first, Tobachischin."

The cave mouth was just a little broader than my shoulders and I eased myself in, feet first, feeling a tangle of roots and rocks against my spine. Once in, the cave was cool. I let myself down; the light above me was swallowed. Into the darkness I dropped, sightless as a mole person. Showers of pebbles fell on my head. And I descended, darkly. Above me were Grandfather's feet, the little pebbles raining down. Then the cave was very wide and there was a finger of white light below, and I came out on a sunlit ledge.

Slithering, I emerged upon it and saw at once that we'd come a great ways down—the arroyo, or dry riverbed, was close. All round it the feathery tops of the salt cedars . . . not far off, the helper hawk, crying. His red-bronze shoulders tilted at my eye level. Then he dropped down, disappearing into the silence of the cedars.

Grandfather said, "We have helpers everywhere, Grandson."

"Should we follow the ledge down?"

He squinted at the bright sun, nodded.

So we went all the way to the bottom. We didn't see the ground squirrel again, but the hawk was close, eyeing us from the cedar. Once, as we lowered ourselves down towards the silver gleam of the arroyo, Grandfather, putting his hand on my shoulder, said, "You're going too fast." Another time he told me, "That rock under your left foot is going to roll, be careful." Sure enough, as soon as I lifted my foot away from that rock, it sprung free, arced into the air, and thudded on the arroyo sand.

When, at last, our toes touched the earth, we looked back up at the tower of stone above us. The vast rock went straight up, soaring into the sky. We drank from the ribbon of water that ran between the banks of the arroyo. Grandfather whispered, "Our relations have seen us through our ordeal so far. Give thanks, Grandson."

Then he dug into his medicine bundle and took out a pinch of cornmeal, which he sang to, blessing it and us with his whisper song. Crouched in the cedars, he sang a gentle prayer, low and into the wind, and afterwards he filled our skin bag full of water. The shade of the cedars was shelter from prying eyes . . . whose? I didn't know but I felt them.

"Does anyone use this part of the canyon?" I asked.

"This is a place of circles that wind into one another. This opens into a smaller canyon, further up. There we'll meet people, if we're not careful. But here, for the moment, we're safe."

We waited for the time of shadows to come, twilight, when things unseen move mutely and secretly. Then, Grandfather held out the walking stick and it shook in the cedar gloom and showed us the way up canyon. I watched as Grandfather placed his feet only on the tops of rocks, never in the water, or the wet sand. As daylight died in the canyon and darkness came, the night crickets called, *criss, criss*, in the willows.

After much walking there was the sharp smell of cedar wood burning. The smoke was pulled downwind and along with it there came the odor of roasting meat. The teasing smoke was afloat on the wind and my mouth was wet with hunger.

Then we heard *Naakaii*: voices husky, full of wine and food. Grandfather plucked at my shoulder, a touch soft as a moth. We had come to a place where many boulders were piled. Peering over the edge of one, I saw a bright beard of flame. My heart jumped against my ribs. Grandfather whispered, "Don't worry, Owl Boy is close by and he will sprinkle some owl medicine, and then no one will see us."

No sooner said than a mottled desert owl flew around our heads. For an instant, he hung suspended in the night-dark with the crickets cricking, and then he went behind the big rocks. Grandfather spoke a silent prayer to the owl's spirit, and told me to follow him into the firelight. We walked, then, unafraid, into the camp of the *Naakaii* bounty hunters.

Two men were awake, the others hunched down, or lying rolled up in their banded serape blankets. We walked into their midst, glancing neither left nor right. The men with their high-crowned, big-brimmed hats tipped at an angle, were snoring. The night guards, who were not asleep, were having a conversation. They had their long rifles in the crook of their arms, and the fire-light glinted on the barrels of the guns as they joked and talked.

As Grandfather had said, we were unseen. The stalk-ing moon was high on the canyon's rim, but the gift of Owl Boy made us invisible and the *Naakaii* guards saw only their own firelit faces.

However, as we reached the outside of the camp, a slumbering man kicked off his blanket. I was between him and Grandfather, and I froze there and the man's open eyes seemed to see me, or into me. He grunted and lay down, and dropped back to sleep. I froze. Noth-ing happened. The guards talked quietly. At last I thought it was safe to move. Grandfather came to me, whispering, "They can't see or hear us . . . watch this." He walked back to the fire pit, around which many men were asleep. He selected a big piece of roasted meat that was hanging from an iron rod. Smiling with satisfaction, he returned without a sound and, touching my elbow, gestured that we should go on.

For a long time we walked in silence under the pointed stars and the high yellow moon. The canyon was broader; we left the bounty camp well behind; and as we went along, I smelled the roasted meat in Grand-father's hand and it made my belly growl. Soon we came up into the smell of juniper scrub, where we were greeted by the warmer air of the desert. The wide, moonlit walls of the canyon were far apart now and we squatted under a twisted tree and ate in silence. The taste of the rich meat was good. A long time it had been since I had had such a taste. When we finished and we were licking our fingers, I asked Grandfather if Owl Boy's medicine was still at work. He shrugged and said, "We don't need him now."

Then I heard the twang of a bowstring and the solid thunk as an arrow buried itself in flesh. Grandfather started to stand, sat down, hunched in the sand. Coming out of his chest was the flint point of an arrow. He sagged to one side, looked piercingly into my eyes.

"Grandson, Two Face wants my medicine bag. You mustn't let him have the coyote bead."

I cradled his head as he struggled to breathe.

"He wants the coyote bead," he said. His lips were barely parted.

"Don't speak, Grandfather."

"You mustn't give him that bead," he sighed. "I've saved it all this time." His breath came short and hard and he made a rattling noise in his throat. Suddenly, his eyes closed and he went limp in my arms.

I slipped off Grandfather's medicine bundle and took up his walking stick. I did not hurry to make my escape. I knelt under the glare of that stalking moon, knowing that I was watched by an evil and cunning eye. Knowing, too, that the one who waited and watched saw me clearly and well. I was there for the taking, or the playing, or whatever it was.

For a moment I breathed the burnt smell of the night-blooming plants. A little ways away a great, moon-colored datura was unfolding in the pale brilliance.

The moon seemed to mock my timid spirit. I glanced hesitantly for a sign of the owl, the one who had helped us before, and under my breath, I chanted the owl song.

> *Owl Brother, Old One*
> *You, whose head has two points*
> *You, who sit on spruce*
> *You, with white smoke*
> *And hooked claws*

You, who protect me with your smoke,
Make me invisible.

I didn't wait, though, to see if the chant worked. Instead, I lay Grandfather on the dry wash of the moon. I removed his moccasins, filled them with sand, pointed them North so he could take the spirit path.

I knew I shouldn't dwell on his death, or what had just happened. Like my parents, his spirit was free, as mine was not. I needed to go on. I needed to get away. Our ways, the living and the dead, were both to the North. But they were separate now. I would miss him, for he, more than anyone, had taught me all that I knew. I hated to leave him there and travel on, alone. But that was how it was.

The cry of the coyote shattered the rimrock night. I ran from it, darting, a lame rabbit seeking shelter that wasn't there. Behind me in the white rocks the coyote's laughter was shrill. I put the cowry shell under my tongue—and started running.

And ran north toward the blue Lukachukai.

The Sound of Falling Hooves

Over my head and shoulder, I slung Grandfather's medicine bag. In my belt I had the knife my father gave me. And, over my other shoulder there was the water skin that bumped musically against my ribs as I ran. These things and of course the walking stick, which I carried in my right hand, were my only possessions.

I knew not what lay ahead—barely did I understand what lay behind. For the moment, I was running, heading north and not resting, just running and breathing, moving across the sparkling sand. Sometime before the moon completed the arc that ends at dawn, my adversary, Two Face, sent me whirlwinds.

Well I understood his ways and though I ran from him, I knew that, sooner or later, I would have to meet him. There was no evading Two Face. Like the desert he was a thing of permanence.

Yet that would not stop me from trying to escape.

When the four whirlwinds came, I saw them from afar—two capes of dust, then two more joining them. They ate at the desert, spewing cactus arms and tumbleweeds in their wake. They were black and malign and they moaned keenly in the hollow distance as they chased after me.

I kept on but so did the whirlwinds, gaining ground faster than I was. Gathering strength, they entwined like four snakes that turn into one. Then, as the night faded into morning, the sky was marred by the ghostly roaring of the circular wind. It clutched the earth from below while its head spun above; dispersing birds and small animals like blown leaves.

Listening with attentive ears for any change in the devil wind's pattern, I decided I had no choice but to stop running. There was nothing I could do but hide. Finding a small white cap of rock in which to wedge myself out of the way of the wind's roar, I got as flat as a blue-tail lizard. The water skin was too large to fit in there with me, so I left it outside and brought only the medicine bag and walking stick.

A fissure, a crack in the earth's flesh, was all it was—yet, for me, it was a chance to survive.

The whirlwind had grown so strong, it sucked up pines and ground them into powder. Trapped, I flattened myself and lay still, listening to the flexing of the air and the crackling spines of sun-dried trees as they were ground up and spat out.

The whirlwind was hunting for me, scouring the sands. Hungrily, it bore down, skirling and crying. This was followed by vicious thunderclaps. From my hiding place under the rock's lip, I saw the three-finger dawn torn apart. Lightning reached down like white roots, whose after-burning brightness stung my eyes.

Shielding them, I pushed my face into the dirt so I wouldn't see anything. Then I covered my ears, while a constant hail of sharp rocks stormed all around me. The whirlwind began to scream. I feared my rock would be lifted and slammed down on top of me, crushing my bones. However, though it scouted the sands, the whirlwind seemed unable to find me.

Then, as suddenly as it started, it stopped. It unraveled in the wind, funneling off thinly into the four-finger morning light. A queer, unsettling silence settled down on the prickly sand. The cicadas, so noisy at daybreak, were gone. Far off a raven coughed and then was still. There was the bark of a fox. A coldness crept out of the sky, pressing down. I started to crawl out of my hiding place when the whirlwind returned—this time with renewed force.

It came with stinging fangs of snow. Half out from under my little ledge, I felt the flakes cut my cheeks. I ducked back. The whirlwind had reshaped itself, but its evil presence was the same, and it wanted me no less than before; and I wondered if I could get away, or whether I would be buried alive.

Hunkering down, I hugged the earth. And into my narrow, shoulder-crushing shelter spun the eager, death-like flakes. The sun rose and the wounded land darkened. The desert hummed, grimly and coldly, layering the landscape with white.

I shivered. In front of my face, to block out the snow, I pushed the medicine bag. Its leather folds protected me, but I could feel the fury of the wind.

I pressed my fingers against the bag. I knew what was in it. A stone arrow straightener, black horsehair whip, porcupine quill comb, red powder for making war paint, and a little white piece of doeskin wrapped around the blue coyote bead. That was all, that was the whole of it—my protection, my medicine. What strange things Grandfather had left me with—of what worth? I shivered but not only from the seeping, creeping cold.

I peeked around the bag outside the crevice; the desert was awhirl in whiteness. My cold enemy was filling the day with white feathers, glittering feathers. In a short time, I was blanketed with snow.

And though I could breathe, the weight on my shoulders and the killing cold held me prisoner. I was stuck to the frozen earth, pinned. And now the snow dimmed the day and turned it dark. I was completely buried alive.

Soon the air began to grow stale. I had to fight to fill my lungs. But the desire was in me to fight, to struggle . . . fighting off the fear that sapped my heart, I did the only thing I knew . . . I reached into the medicine bag.

My hand closed around the first thing I felt: the arrow straightener.

Bringing it out of the bag, I said, "Grandfather, that which worked for you shall work for me." With this small stone implement, I started chopping against the bank of snow.

The white wall began to melt. Swiftly I dug myself out of my frozen grave, and wherever I touched that arrow straightener, the snow withdrew, melting and steaming. I was soon standing out in the four-finger dawn light, breathing the delicious air. Alive, oh, I was alive!

"Thank you, Grandfather," I said, and put away the arrow straightener. Now I knew what it was and how it could be used; yet, in haste, I raised the walking stick, and it bent towards the Lukachukai. North and away from the warm, turning from the sun that graced my back, I ran. For the time being, the whirlwind was gone.

I trotted into the drifts, the cowry under my tongue, the medicine bag over my shoulder. At my feet the snow turned into silver.

At midday I stopped and built a small fire under a wind-bent salt cedar. The wood of this tree makes hardly any smoke. The steel gray sky cleared as I warmed my wet feet. I looked around, wondering what would come my way. The country was cliffrose and juniper, and shiny slivers of running water. The banded land lay like a purple blanket, smoking in the sun haze. At the end of the desert the long blue, big-shouldered mountains awaited me, offering sanctuary, if I could get to them.

After warming myself I snuffed out the fire, covered it with sand. The snow was melting, but I knew that if I ran on it, I would leave tracks that could be followed by a blind magpie. Clearly, Two Face hadn't wanted me dead; he had wanted me alive. He was saving me, I thought. The way a coyote saves a wounded rabbit—by walking, not running, after it. I stared at the white glitter, the snow-tufted mesas.

I put the walking stick before me, watched it point north where it held course, straight and sure.

After going a good distance from the salt cedar place, I arrived at the edge of a cliff. Down into another canyon I went.

Behind me the sun shone, glazing the desert with a fine, bright skin of glitter water. My tracks would soon be melted away in the runoff. Thankfully, I sat on my haunches and sang the sun chant. I praised Sun Father's turquoise horse, whose hooves strike fire on the clouds; whose muscled flesh is misty and agleam with pollen. Chanting, I stared at the sky. The great blue horse of the sun pounded out of the shallow pink cloud banks. I closed my eyes and continued to sing. The sound of falling hooves drummed louder, a sudden warmth fanned my face.

Opening my eyes, I saw that the sun had burnished the desert into sheets of flaming copper. No one could follow me through such a glare.

I sang the sun song again.

> I am the Sun's son
> I sit upon a turquoise horse
> At the opening of the sky
> My horse walks on terrifying hooves
> And stands at the upper circle of the rainbow
> With a sunbeam in his mouth for a bridle
> My horse circles all the people of the earth
> Today I ride on his broad back and he is mine
> Tomorrow he will belong to another

I heard then the whinnying of the wind.

And made my way down into the rainbow belly of the canyon.

Hodoogani, Land of Massacre

With my descent into the canyon the rainbow whispered away. This was a bad sign. Something was wrong. Something in the wind. I sensed the breath of a *chindi*, a ghost. I moved more rapidly, always heading north. But I saw nothing; I kept on the move, restless and uneasy.

Presently I came to a curve in the canyon. At the foot of a steep cliff, there were tumbled rocks. In the rubble, I saw what was troubling me. Among the rust-colored rocks were the bodies of *Dineh*. Men and women: crushed, broken, and dead. Their red and blue leggings were still bright, but their faces were twisted.

I didn't wonder what had driven them off the cliff—for I knew. The dead, their mouths open in an agony of silence, told all there was to tell. We call such a haunted place *hodoogani*, "Land of Massacre." It was bad for me to be there; bad for me to be thinking about it.

The lost *chindi* would confuse my way. They might follow me, perhaps taunt with me with their mad dreams.

The dead, as we know, go to that underground place, where the caves are. There they make up their mind what animal they want to be in the next lifetime. After this they travel North, underground. And come out of the caves, finally, free to be what they want to be—owls, eagles, wolves, and bears, and even little thirteen-lined ground squirrels. Yes, all these are people we have once known and loved, friends and family. Which is why we always call them animal persons.

I hobbled out of there fast, not looking back.

That day, I ran until evening. Then, after resting for a time, I continued on. Always moving, never glancing over my shoulder to see if anyone was following. Thus did I run until I was too tired to go on any farther.

Toward dusk I came to a black rock place where the sand was like old dried blood. This was one of those ancient burial grounds called The Blood of the Giant. Long ago Elder Brother slew many evil monsters. In death, their blood ran over the earth. Such places have been purified by time, but we still say our prayers over them, to cast away the spirit of death.

All round lay the dark, porous stones that are good for heating and for making sweat baths. I needed to eat and drink, and to rest—but just as important was the need to cleanse myself. So here I made camp and gathering the blood rocks, I built a cedar fire. When the rocks glowed from the fire's heat, I lifted them out with two sticks and put them into a natural stone bowl of snowmelt. The cavity was just deep enough to fit my tired body into.

After putting nine hot rocks into the bath, I took off my sweat-soaked deerskin shirt, removed my loincloth and my moccasins. The water was scalding hot; I lowered myself in. Then I grabbed at some sage that grew close by and mixed that into the bath, too.

Night came down the canyon as I soaked and the warmth went into my tired bones. Darkness settled softly like a star-woven velvet. My aches went away; I drifted in and out of sleep, watching the flickering of the first stars in the great blanket of night. I lay still for a long while, finally getting out of the bath and into the bracing cool air. Now I rubbed tufts of sage all over my arms and legs. After this I waded into the icy stream that ran nearby.

Cold fire cut into my loins, and then something sleek touched my knee. Smooth like silk, I felt it. Three times it touched me. The fourth time I snapped my hand into the stream and grabbed a shining trout. I caught two of them this way with open hand. And brought them to my fire pit and cooked them in their silver skins on the coals.

When the trout were starting to split apart, I ate them. After a while I built up the fire. With some of the warm ash, I made a poultice for my leg. Then I drank from the icy stream until my teeth ached from the cold.

In the darkness of the tinkling trout stream, I heard a heron croak. It broke out of the red willows and flew overhead, coming down out of the starry air to land in the place it had just left. I heard the gray wings fanning and chopping, as he steadied himself on the willow branch. *Grawk, grawk*, came his night cry. A good sign, Grandfather told me that the heron is our guardian. From the first days of life, the heron helped us to find the lands of light, the sun country.

I felt safe with the heron near and the stream singing on its bed of stones, the stars sharp and close. Clutching my medicine bag, I drifted in and out of sleep, dreaming, not dreaming, coming awake, slipping into sleep again on the fire-warmed sand under the burning stars. Just before the first finger of dawn, I had good luck—my eyes opened and there was a rock dove, which I killed with a well-aimed pebble. This precious bird I gave thanks for, roasting and eating it for my morning's meal. Out of the willows my guardian heron, heavy-winged and weighted with dew, thrust itself up into the chilly sky. I watched him fly away, croaking, his big wings pounding the air. As he turned towards the south, I thanked him for guarding me all through the night.

For the rest of the morning, I walked along the tricky, full-throated stream, and in time came upon a trail used by sheep and sheepherders. Among the damaged cliffrose, broken and hanging down, I found a bunch of bright-eyed yellow sunflowers. Some had seeds the birds had missed, and I ate them hungrily for my midday meal.

When the seeds were gone, I followed the sheep tracks. Once, another heron flew near beating its wings protectively over my head. As always, I used my walking stick to see if I was going in the right direction; and it gestured north towards the Lukachukai Mountains, now hovering into view. The sheep trail was going that way too, so I followed it for the rest of the afternoon.

The cliffs glittered and guttered with snowmelt. The sheep trail was slippery—too dangerous to walk on any longer. So I scaled the canyon wall. I climbed up into the setting sun. On top I found myself in an open prairie. The sheep camp was close.

I walked under *piñon* trees on a field of beaten sage. The sheep I smelled—even before seeing them. Huddled in a corral of straight juniper poles, their coats were all dirty and wet from the snow. Where there were sheep there were herders, whose tracks I'd seen earlier—but where were they? I hid myself behind a tree and suddenly the earth thrummed with hoofbeats and four riders galloped up. They were Utes; hard, bear-like men with black woolen coats that hung down to their ankles. Mounted on lean-muscled horses, each man carried a rifle but not the kind *Dineh* had—the Ute guns were shorter and lighter and easier to hold.

As I peeked around the tree, the Utes started firing their guns. There was a shelter, the kind used by *Bilagaana,* white people. A tent, Grandfather had once called it, in American. Around it the Utes paraded foolishly, kicking up dust, shouting and shooting. They fired into the open ends of the tent. From inside there was a terrible noise like mourning women make after someone's been killed.

A white woman ran out of the tent with two children in her arms. One of the Utes threw himself from his horse, walked towards her while she screamed at him. Her shoulder was red with blood. The Ute reached for his knife and casually thrust it into her shirt-front. The woman dropped; the Ute laughed in his throat. The children tried to run away, but another man captured them and tied bags over their heads. After binding their hands, he beat them with the butt of his rifle.

The sheep camp was full of the noises of the sheep, the stomping of the horses, the crying of the *Bilagaana* children. Still hidden, I watched the Utes ransack the tent. They dragged things out into the open, pitching them all about. Finding sacks of goods that they liked, they mounted their snorting horses and rode off with the children. I waited for some time in the gathering darkness before I slipped out from behind the tree.

It was almost dark. I crept about to see if the Utes had forgotten anything. They had—in their haste. There was a metal box, inside of which I found the hard, dry

berries that the *Bilagaana* crush and boil into a hot drink.
I ate a few of these but they were very bitter and I spat
them out. On the ground I saw the white sand that is
used for sweetness. A lot of this was spilled around and I
ate it off the ground like a deer.

After this I sniffed the ground for more of the sweet
sand, but there wasn't any. The white woman lay dead
in the starlight. I did not go near her. Then I heard a
loud crack. And felt in my ribs the sting of a scorpion.
Someone had shot me; warm blood ran down my side
and into my groin. I couldn't see who had done it. But I
heard the laugh of a coyote. I took two steps and blacked
out.

Mary's Eyes

When I opened my eyes I found myself at my old camp on The Blood of the Giant. I tried to sit up, couldn't—the pain was too great. I lay there wondering who—or what—had brought me back to this place. The last thing I remembered was the crack of the rifle, the bullet biting into me, and then the hot blood. Feeling my ribs I discovered the wound was dressed in a soft bandage. Who had done this?

I was propped against a willow-woven backrest. Someone had put a sheepskin over it . . . who?

The sky was cold and clear. Late morning, I knew that much. In my old fire pit the coals were idly smoking . . . was this now the camp of my enemies, the Utes? I glanced about for some evidence of *Nooda'i*, the murdering Utes, who'd killed the *Bilagaana* woman and stolen her children. The camp offered no sign of them, but then a beautiful young *Dineh* appeared on the bank of the stream. She wore a loose deerskin skirt that covered all but her knee-high moccasins. With her hair braided in flannel, she could've passed for a Ute, but I knew she wasn't . . . the shape of her face, large and oval, was ours, not theirs. However, she'd been a captive; of that I was certain, which explained her Ute hair. All this I saw in a few seconds.

I was not quite over my surprise when I heard a baby cry. Turning my head, I saw a cradleboard. The child was shaded from the sun by a well-placed salt bush branch. Inside the folds of sheepfur, the baby's eyes glistened darkly. They were laughing eyes—and surprisingly—not black but light brown. The skin, too, was pale white shell, which made me think the baby was neither *Naakaii* nor *Nooda'i*—but *Bilagaana*.

What strangeness, what beauty . . .

I watched the woman as she fed the baby cornmeal mush from a gourd. After a little while, she came over, knelt beside me. Her eyes were black as flint. "You're comfortable?" she asked, in Navajo. I nodded, said nothing. Even her voice was pretty to hear.

She said, "I am called Mary." A small smile crept across her lips, but quickly faded.

"What clan do you belong to?" I asked, thinking I might know it.

"Red Streak Reaching Water."

"I know the *Tachii'nii*. Some of your people lived not far from us." I paused and then added, "Why do you call yourself by a *Bilagaana* name?"

She frowned; her dark, quick eyes found mine, then darted away. I'd never seen eyes so beautiful.

"Our family was rounded up, taken to *Hweeldi*," she said bitterly. "I do not need to tell you how horrible it was there, or how many people died, or why things happened the way they did. Or what it was like going to *Hweeldi* when so many died walking. Surely you know these things, have heard stories. But maybe you don't know why they made us go there in the first place."

She talked like her eyes moved, fast. It was the way the *Bilagaana* talk.

"Tell me what happened; I've heard nothing."

She looked at me curiously.

"Where have you been all this time?"

"In hiding."

"Well, this is my story—it is like this. They told us, the *Bilagaana* did, that we *Dineh* were living too far apart. They said we weren't civilized, we weren't settled. They said we were wild animals and they told us that there were other Indians like us, who now farmed peacefully at *Halgai Hatkeel*."

"Where is that?"

"The blue coats call it *Oklah-Homah*. A name given by some other tribe of Indians . . . Cherokees."

"Is that the end?"

She gave me a funny look.

". . . I mean of your story."

"No," she said. "There is more, but I don't feel like talking so much now; maybe later, if you still want to listen. Are you hungry?"

I told her that I was and she stood up and inspected the baby, who was now asleep. "I have a little sheep's milk that I've been keeping cold in the stream, and some blue cornmeal. This is what I feed the baby—and myself. But the milk's about finished."

"I ate two fish from this stream yesterday," I told her.

She touched my face; her hand was cold.

"You're hot from the fever in your wound. The bullet went through you clean, but the wound is deep and will take some time to heal. You must use herbs to get the bad medicine out of your body."

"Are you a medicine woman?" I asked.

"I know some things," she answered, bending down and helping me to my feet. She was stronger than she looked. How easily she got my arm over her shoulders and walked me to the bathing place I'd found the day before. Steam rose in plumes off the heated pool. She'd heated it the way I had, using the blood stones of the giant.

"I'm not able to fit in there," I said. "It hurts when I double up."

Smiling, she answered, "The water's not for bathing—it's for drinking."

I looked at her questioningly. "Drinking?"

"*Deetjaad*," she said seriously.

I knew what she meant: the wild herbs Grandfather used to purify himself.

"I thought it was just an old man's drink because Grandfather used it."

"Now you are the old man." She smiled again.

"I suppose I am at that." Her eyes flashed darkly; no doubt, she was the prettiest woman I'd ever seen.

"What we must do," she explained, "is get the bad blood out of you. The herbs in this hot water will do this thing."

She helped me kneel to the ground. I realized that I was wearing a clean loincloth. Embarrassed, I knew she'd changed me when she dressed my wound. So I was an old man, and a helpless one. And I hadn't even the strength to cup the water to my mouth. Using a gourd dipper, she brought it to my lips, saying, "Go ahead, drink and get well."

So I drank and the hot, bitter water was awful in my mouth—worse when I swallowed. I wanted to retch but she wouldn't let me; she made me drink more. Then she got a sage stick from the fire pit, and made me breathe in the sweet smoke. That was good and it cleared my head.

After this she put a burning sprout of sage in the hot water and put a handful over my open wound. The pain was great: I closed my eyes, clenched my teeth. In my mind I went somewhere away from the pain. I rode the sun horse, rode him high in the sky.

When I came back out of the clouds, the teeth-clenching pain was still there, but there, too, was this lovely Mary. After a while, she wrapped a band of deer-skin around the wound, binding it well for support. I thanked her.

Then my belly growled and I felt my bowels unloos-ening all of a sudden. "I have to be by myself," I told her and she helped me hobble out of sight of the camp. Then, when she was gone, thunder broke inside me. What came out and stained the earth was red, dark red—the bad blood of the bullet gushing out of me. Moments later I stood up, shakily, the sweat running off my face. Then I cleaned myself thoroughly.

However, I couldn't walk back to the camp, I was too weak. Calling for Mary, I rested against a rock, feeling helpless and foolish and tired. When she came, bringing my walking stick, I tried to smile, saying, "That is not what you think it is."

"What is it then?" she asked.

"Magic," I said. "Grandfather's medicine."

Looking steadily at me for the first time, she asked my name.

"I am called Tobachischin." She nodded, lifted me up, with my arm around her shoulder, and walked me back to the fire pit.

"It is a good name but how is it," she asked, "that you

are named after a god? Tobachischin is the younger brother of Nayenazgani, the Monster Slayer."

I gritted my teeth. "Don't you think I know that?"

"I'm sorry." She helped me lie against the willow backrest. "My grandfather was a great medicine man," I told her. "He named me."

"Would I know of him?"

I shook my head. "The People didn't want his Ways. He knew the Coyote Bead Ceremony and he said he would teach it to everyone, but *Dineh* wanted to make war instead. So Grandfather went away and he took me with him. He lived on top of Canyon del Muerto, in complete seclusion."

"And that is what saved you?"

"Yes. But he didn't make it."

"And the rest of your family—?"

I made the cutoff sign—hands crossing, canceling.

Mary gave me some water to drink and some corn-meal and a little sheep's milk.

"I owe you my life," I told her.

Mary's eyes darted away like a canyon wren.

"Maybe . . . if it wasn't for me," she stammered, fumbling with her hands, "you wouldn't be . . . hurt at all."

"What does that mean?"

She frowned and sighed and looked at the chuckling stream, glinting in the sun.

"I was the one who shot you."

"You?" I eyed her wonderingly and now with suspicion. "How is that possible?"

"I had a long gun."

"I wasn't armed," I protested. Still, I couldn't believe she was telling me the truth. Yet why would she lie?

"You were stealing our things. I thought you were a Ute."

"What things?" Now I knew she was telling the truth. It was in her eyes.

"I saw you crawling around in the darkness, eating the little black beans."

"For the loss of them, you would've killed a *Dineh,* one of your own people?"

She didn't answer. She placed a sheepskin over my bare legs.

"Are you warm enough, Tobachischin?"

"I feel a little coldness in me now." I thought to myself: how strange—she hurts me, she heals me. Did I look so much like a Ute? Then I remembered how I'd thought she was one, at first glance . . . her hair. Did I, too, resemble one of those cruel marauders? Perhaps, I thought, perhaps.

Then the world went dark and the knife point of the shrinking sky became a speck and I spun away into the huge night, trying to grab onto something . . . and remembered Mary's eyes.

The Man Called Tall Mountain

When I woke the sun was at five fingers, halfway across the sky. I was stretched out on the fire-warmed sand, feeling a lot better. Mary was feeding the baby cornmeal and stream water. The sun was touching the tops of the trees, the wind rustling the leaves of the little oaks. Down canyon the song of a wren trickling down the high, dry air. For some time I watched the white-trimmed wings of a vulture as it flew back and forth across the cliffs. Pain notwithstanding, I was deeply at peace. As if my mother and father and grandfather were alive again; as if we were not at war, as if it were another time entirely. *Hozhoni*, that feeling of being at ease with all that is, had now come back into my life. And I had Mary to thank for it, even if she was the one who had mistakenly shot me. Somehow, I sensed this little canyon wasn't a place the Utes liked.

Nor did the blue coats come there, for there was no sign of them.

We were alone, the three of us, and it reminded me of the *hozhoni* feeling on top of Grandfather's mesa.

After she fed the little one, Mary told me her about her trail of sorrow. "I was stolen," she said, while sewing my ragged, bullet-pierced shirt. The *Naakaii* captured me a year ago and sold me as a *yisnaah*, a slave. I escaped from that hacienda, but I was caught by Two Face's four Utes. They turned me in to the blue coats, who marched me and a lot of others to *Hweeldi*."

For a time, she said nothing. She sewed my shirt with rapt eyes and with her hand rising and dipping in the cicada-singing afternoon. I waited for her to go on. She finally did. "The soldiers punished me terribly at *Hweeldi*. But I was treated no worse than the other *Dineh* there. We hadn't any warm clothes and when the cold weather came our provisions were gone and our clothes were ragged. Many of the women and children died of starvation. All of us were sick. I was one of the lucky ones who lived."

I thought she was finished talking, but she put another piece of deer sinew through the bone-awl needle she was using, and began her story again.

"What happened to the men?" I wanted to know.

"They had to fight the Comanches," she said.

"Comanches? We were not at war with them."

"You know them?"

"I know they are strong fighters, but what were they doing at *Hweeldi*?"

Mary went on with her sewing as she explained. "The blue coats paid the Comanches in store goods to raid our camp and kill as many of us as possible. Our men knew the government cattle would soon be gone. They knew there would be no more food. So during the day they went out to snare rabbits and prairie dogs. When they were out just a little ways from our camp, the Comanches came and killed them. Then they went off as if nothing had happened. We lost most of our men that way."

"Didn't the blue coats stop them?"

Mary gave me a surprised stare. "Are you not listening to me? The blue coats paid them to do this. Besides, some *Dineh* wanted to die in this manner. For to be killed by a warrior's lance was better than to waste away in sickness. The Comanches understood what they were doing and the blue coats made it worth their while."

Mary broke off and continued her sewing in silence. Finally, I asked, "Was there no food after that?"

"We had those little dark beans that you found in the sheep camp. We crushed them and made a paste of them. This we mixed with *Bilagaana* flour."

I changed my position in the sand and I saw a red-tailed hawk swoop low and settle on a limb. Mary continued, "We made the beans into cakes, but this tasted worse." She laughed.

"They are very bitter," I said, smiling and remembering. "That is why the *Bilagaana* like them."

Mary continued. "Then came an old grandmother, who had been a slave of the *Naakaii*. She knew things we didn't. She showed us how to boil the little dark beans and make them into a hot drink. With much sugar, it tasted all right."

"Can you make some?" I asked.

She chuckled, "Yes, I can make it."

Then, remembering something else, her lips tightened.

I waited, watched. Her eyes were lost in memory.

"I don't hate them," she told me.

"The *Bilagaana*?"

She nodded, finishing a stitch. Then she bit off the end of the sinew, and tied the strands with her fingers. She put my shirt on a log by the fire and smoothed it out with her hands.

"It is hard to explain this . . . you see, they are my second family. My *Dineh* family died long before *Hweeldi*. I saw the last of our clan perish there, but my mother and father, my aunts and uncles were killed by the Utes when I was much younger. We never hated the Americans; we never called them '*eyoni*, or enemy, until *Hweeldi*. But, even then, it was the Utes and the Comanches we hated the most."

I said, "The blue coats bought the Utes, paying them just like the Comanches. Our family hated anyone that tried to make slaves of us. They are all '*eyoni*."

Mary shook her head. "No," she insisted softly. "You have it wrong. *Dineh* always fought against the *Nooda'i*. They are our real enemies. They, not the blue coats, destroyed my family. But now I want to tell how I escaped from *Hweeldi*, how I got my second family."

She put a piece of black oak on the fire and the flames crackled and gripped the log with eager fingers.

On the other side of the stream, the red-tail called with a cry as sharp as its eye. The sky lowered and the day dwindled. Shadows stole across the sand.

Mary went on and I listened.

"There was a man, a sheepherder who supplied our camp at *Hweeldi*. His name was *Hastin Dzit Nineez*. I called him 'Tall Mountain' because that's where he found me after I ran away."

"How far did you get away from *Hweeldi*?"

"I left one night, running. I never stopped until I came to the mountains. There are some high mountains in that country. And there was a road leading into them.

A wagon with a soft roof came along that road, and I climbed into the back of it and hid myself there. At night when the wagon stopped, I got out and found shelter out of sight. Then in the morning, I ate whatever scraps were left by the fire. Then I ran and caught up to the wagon, and got inside it again. That way, I traveled all through the mountains and out the other side and across the plain, all the way to here."

"You came far," I said, admiring her for her courage. "No man could've done better."

She smiled quickly, then grew serious. "Once I got here, I knew where I was and I lived in the canyons far from anyone—for I trusted no one. Not even *Dineh*. I ate wild grass seeds and wood rats. I shed my torn *biil'ee*, my dress. I killed a deer and made the clothes you see me wearing. When it was cold and game was scarce, I ate burned corn and rotten peaches in the ruined fields. Even the birds wouldn't touch what I ate. Once, I saw Two Face himself burning a field of corn. When he was gone, I went there and ate the blackened cobs. I sucked on the cobs and the ravens sang all around me. One night I was hiding in a tree."

The hawk was opening its wings and glaring as if it too were listening, and wanted to hear more.

"I was going to spend the night in the tree, just like that hawk," Mary continued. "But some wild *Bilagaana* dogs came after me. They started to paw at the tree trunk. One of them was big like a wolf, and he kept jumping up to where I was. He almost caught me with his snapping teeth, but I was too quick for him. I had a stick to strike his face when he jumped. He didn't like that, but he kept coming for me. I was very scared."

Mary got up and went to the cradleboard. The baby was still fast asleep. Returning, she told me, "I got tired of fighting off that big dog. Soon I was no longer hitting back, but just holding on to the trunk of the tree, and trying to keep my feet up high. I was bitten a few times before Tall Mountain came. He's the one I told you about. He fired his rifle, scared away the dog pack. Then he asked me to come down out of the tree. My foot was bleeding, so I came down."

"Tall Mountain was *Bilagaana*; his wife, too. Her name was Mary and their baby is Mary too."

"Too many Marys," I said, putting a little twig into the fire.

"Tall Mountain named me Hootsoh Mary."

"Green Meadow Mary . . . well, it suits you," I laughed.

I wondered if Tall Mountain was one of those traders who could talk *Dineh* and I asked her about it. She said, "He was a trader; he knew many ways of speaking." As she spoke a chill came into the canyon and it rustled the brittle leaves of the small oaks. I gathered the sheepskin around me.

"What happened to Tall Mountain?" I asked.

Her eyes dropped, her lips thinned.

"Two Face killed him," she replied, her face flushing with sudden anger. "He killed Big Mary, too. The gods were with me when I saved Little Mary, but that was the only blessing of that day."

"Two Face killed my grandfather." Her eyes met mine.

After a moment's silence, I added, "One day . . . I will meet him . . . and it will be different."

Suddenly Mary's face tightened.

"I don't want to lose you," she said, her lower lip trembling. Then, embarrassed by her sudden feelings, she looked away. I watched her as she filled gourds with water from the stream. "You won't lose me," I said to myself. "And I won't lose you." But though I said it with my heart, I wondered if it were true.

The Coyote Bead

That night I heard the owls, and they reminded me, and I saw Grandfather again. His startled face, his dying eyes. And I vowed that I wouldn't rest until the 'eyoni Ute was dead. I had magic in my medicine bag and my frailty was temporary. I'd soon recover—I had to. I slept and dreamed, but my dreams were violent and troublesome, and full of strangeness.

The dawn came and with it a blessing of corn pollen given to the four directions. Mary sprinkled some on the top of my head. I did the same for her, and then we each passed the little grains on to the earth, whom we call Changing Woman.

The morning began with wild onions. Mary found them and then while hunting she saw "Old Man Bear," *Schicheii Shash* we call him, or "Grandfather Bear." He's the one who brought coughing and unruly ways. But he's also a healer, a person of much good luck. This morning he didn't cough; he regarded Mary with his small eyes. Then he showed her where the deer were hiding in the willows. She took one with her bow and brought it back to camp. We sang the deer song and the bear song. Mary cut some meat from the deer's haunch and put it on the fire coals scented with sage. We ate that sweet meat in silence, chewing slowly, thankfully. It had been a while since I had eaten anything that good.

The day after I felt strong enough to walk around the camp. My strength was coming back. My blood felt good, my heart strong. Mary saw Grandfather Bear again. This time he showed her a bee's nest in the burl of an oak. We ate honey by the handful that day. Later in the evening Mary discovered many cattail bulbs and, saving some for our supper, she gave the rest to Grandfather Bear as a gift. How long had it been since I'd had deer broth and honey? And eaten the tasty white meat of the cattail?

Gratefully, I sang the bear song Grandfather had taught me.

> *A foot*
> *A foot with toes*
> *A foot with toes came.*
> *He came with a foot with toes*
> *Old Man with your five-toed foot just like ours.*

Mary hadn't heard this one and she asked me to sing it again so she could learn the words. I taught her and we sang it together as the red willows bent in the sunlight in the canyon wind.

But these soft canyon days were done. We needed to move on, and I was ready to do so. Tucking the cowry into my mouth, I started out. We came up out of the canyon, Mary and me and Little Mary. The yellow afternoon greeted us and a feeling of *hozhoni* filled us with courage. The walking stick told us the direction of the Lukachukai Mountains. But now we could almost see them; hazy and huge, faint blue and flower-like in the distance. We could feel them as well; their heart beat in the soles of our feet.

Coming out of the canyon we went far afield of the bad sheep camp. We circled around it and seeing no one, nor any sheep, just the old ruined wagon, we went on. I asked if that wagon was the one that belonged to Tall Mountain, and Mary said it was. I knew it was not polite to ask her how he had come to die unless she wanted to tell me.

It was dusk, the time of deception, when shadows thicken. I showed Mary what was in Grandfather's bag then. "There is much medicine here, things that I don't yet know how to use. When their time comes, they will show me what it is to be done with them." I spread the contents of the bag on a flat rock in the dying sunlight. She looked curiously at the stone arrow straightener, the black horsehair whip, the porcupine quill comb, the bag of red paint dust.

"Where did this come from?" Mary asked, pointing to the porcupine comb.

"From somewhere far to the north. Grandfather was a great trader. He knew what was valuable, too."

"What is inside the wrapping of deerskin?"

I took up the tiny bundle with the coyote bead in it. Now I carefully undid the doeskin covering in the last light of the sun. The blue bead was revealed.

"Do you know the meaning of it?" I asked Mary.

She said, "I think it is for the Coyote Bead Ceremony." Glancing questioningly, she looked at me, to see if I knew.

It was, in fact, the one thing Grandfather had talked about; he'd told me it was the most powerful medicine of all.

I explained, "This blue bead was meant for the mouth of a coyote pup, a male. There is another bead, a white one, that goes into another pup's mouth, a female."

Mary asked, "Where is the white bead?"

I shook my head. "All that was here . . . *is* here. Nothing's been lost."

Mary said, "We'll find the lost white bead."

I looked into her eyes. Where did she get her courage?

She told me, "At *Hweeldi* there was a medicine man. He told me once that Coyote was a very bad person who stole many things, including the stars, long, long ago. He said Coyote was the one responsible for what was happening to us. He said in bad times Coyote makes war. In good times he makes peace."

Grandfather had also told me that, so I knew it was true.

"There is more," I explained to Mary. "When Coyote stole Water Monster's children, the Great Flood wiped out the world. Grandfather said that the same kind of dark ways are with Coyote today. And that's what gives Two Face his power to destroy: he has Coyote."

"There is no sorcery more wicked," Mary agreed.

I wrapped up the blue bead and put away the other things. Then I tied the medicine bag, drawing the string tight, knotting it. "We must find our camp," I said. "It's getting late."

Mary nodded, glancing at the silver sage flats. In the distance where the sun met the horizon, the sky was crimson. I sang a prayer to the Sun Horse. In my mind's eye, I saw him, his flint hooves showering sparks across the iron clouds.

The darkness came and in its afterglow we made our camp by a fallen cottonwood. Nearby, a tangle of wild roses with blossoms brown and gold. There was also a sinkhole of greenish, cloudy water. It looked poor but it tasted all right.

Mary ground the cattail bulbs into paste, mixed them with the last of the *Bilagaana* flour and a little cornmeal. From all of these, she made flat bread that she put on the hot rocks. I tended the bread while she gathered yucca and cactus fruit. Afterward, we ate in silence, Little Mary cooing like a dove. She'd had her own supper of water and meal, and now she was content, moving her hands rapidly as she watched the sky change color and the nighthawks dive.

Wood doves sang in the cottonwoods and Little Mary sounded exactly like them. I listened to the deeper song of the nighthawks, their buzzing, open-mouthed descent in the purple twilight. Here there were ground owls, combing the meadows and chittering, bobbing heads at us from their burrows.

I looked at my moccasins—they were worn to shreds. Mary promised to make me a pair of yucca sandals the next day. "We can hide here tomorrow," she said. "We have plenty of deer jerky. But we need milk for Little Mary."

I finished the crackly thin flat bread.

Locust, singing in the darkness, told me that no matter how dark it is the light will come. Old Locust, Grandfather had said, bent his black bow and loosed a bright arrow into the upper dome of daylight. Thus we *Dineh* came out of the night country, out of the underworld. So would we—Mary, Little Mary, and I—rise to the clear light of morning and be blessed by another day.

That night I dreamed a strange and beautiful dream.

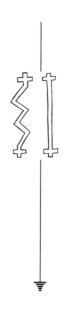

Yellow Eyes

We walked into the shadows, the three of us disappearing, melting.

A coyote howled drunkenly at the moon.

We stared into a pool of water.

Down in the depths, I saw the green face of the old horned one, Water Monster.

Chindi sang in the junipers, telling of ancient arrow-wounds.

The sun rose and set; no horses were seen, no hooves were heard.

I wore a long loincloth that touched the grass at my feet.

I had on the sandals Mary made for me.

"Will you run?" Mary asked. "Will you run for me?"

I glanced round, saw other young men like myself.

It was Mary's race, her woman's time had come, I had to run to win her.

My leg was weak, the bone hurt. My chest ached where the bullet had burned it.

I was not yet strong enough; I looked fearfully at the line of tough young men.

The dawn sun came. Mary ran into it, the light parting like a blanket.

Towards the east we—the others and myself—ran after Mary.

She was a white deer, swift and sure.

I felt myself elbowed out of the race.

A man with a scar that divided his face struck me with a club, I went down tumbling.

I felt myself fractured in the wind, torn by Raven's beak.

I drew on the powers of my medicine.

I became a mote of dust, floating down the smoke hole of a hogan.

Inside round the fire's glow, the scar-faced winner was sharing the wedding corn cake with Mary.

He was eating the circle out of the center.

Laughing with eyes of yellow moons.

In the west corner of the hogan I saw a blue bead.

In the east corner I saw a white bead.

I wanted to do something, but I was merely a mote of dust.

I was undone. Useless, bodiless, and at last, dreamless.

Sparks Flashed, Horses Tumbled

When I awoke in the dark before dawn, Mary was making my sandals. She'd stripped the yucca leaves and had woven soles of them. Strips of deer hide went across my foot in front and between my first and second toes. She worked quickly by firelight, and by sunrise, she was done.

"How did you do it without measuring my foot?"

"I did that while you slept," she said, grinning.

The sandals felt firm on my feet and I knew that I could run far with them. I decided we should go. We said our prayers to the coming sun, ate deer jerky for breakfast. We broke camp, filled our fire pit, and used a juniper bough to cover our tracks until we were some distance away.

The walking stick wiggled toward the west. By mid-day Mary recognized the country we were coming into; she'd been here once before. She called it *Todaa'ni'deetiin*, "Trail-That-Crosses-the-Edge-of-the-Water." The riverbed was dry, so we walked in the hot sun until we came to another place where Mary said, "This is *Seibikooh*, 'Sandy Wash'." In the near distance the mountains seemed close enough to touch. We rested halfway there by the place Mary called *Tse'iiahi*, "Standing Rock."

There was one there, too, a great sentinel stone that soared up into the sky. The foothills here were full of autumn sunflowers. We ate plentifully of their seeds, and I found a medicine man's *mano*, the tool that is used to grind up herbs, under a rough-bark juniper. I left it where I found it, and walked on.

As the afternoon wore on, Little Mary began to cry. There was nothing to give her, so Mary wetted a stick of jerky, softening it with her teeth. This she put in the baby's mouth and it soon dried her tears. "How is your side?" Mary asked me. "Is it hurting?" I told her that I felt all right, and I did; though there was still a dull ache.

In the tawny, panther grass that lay between us and the Lukachukai Mountains, I saw the bone-white skulls of deer and antelope. Over our heads ravens sawed at the air with their heavy black wings. Far off, thunder. Like distant cannons. The sun was swamped in cloud, but no rain came—just long, low threatening shadows that went over us.

"I don't like the feel of this," I said to Mary.

The walking stick wiggled in my hands, pointing as ever toward the breast of the blue mountains.

We trudged on and came to the low scrub pine country that is always before the land of big pines. Occasionally, a hawk dived. Once, a magpie, cackling and chortling. The underside of the little oak leaves fanned up in the air. Again I told Mary that I didn't like the feeling of this wind. She nodded and folded her arms, glancing at the omen-filled, leaden sky. "It will be better in the mountains," she said.

We walked well into the evening. In the burnt dusk, bats fluttered, telling us there was a cave somewhere near. We found water, a throbbing, full-banked stream, and drank our fill. A badger was drinking there, too, and when he saw us, he looked up, white-throated, black-faced. Beady-eyed, he gruffly gave up his place and waddled away, grunting.

Then all of a sudden, a swirl of yellow warblers, whipping before the wind. That was a certain sign of danger. "We'd better find cover," I told Mary. As we began to trot off, following the river bend, I smelled something crisp in the air. Mary caught it, too. Fire—bunch grass burning before a driving blast of rising, wind-driven air. Quail drummed up, bursting and scared, filling the sky with their popping wings.

A sheet of orange flame rose eerily out of nowhere and wrapped the prairie on all sides. Wind whipped and mad, it came roaring after us, eating everything in its path. Juniper trees and scrub pines boomed into flame. Hot flakes of flying ash stormed. We got them in our hair as we jogged into the deep stream. Embers raced over us like shooting stars. The whole night was on fire.

Holding Little Mary's cradleboard up over my head, I took on the fighting current of the creek and made it to the other side. Mary was slower but she soon joined me, panting hard from her sidelong, sweeping swim. It seemed safer on this side, but the fire was following us. Could it overleap the river? We weren't going to wait to find out.

"Is there not something you can do?" Mary asked.

I patted Grandfather's medicine bag.

"We must see what our enemy does first." There was

no doubt in my mind that Two Face was the force behind the flames. On the other side of the river, the red fingers, turning into claws, ripped at the night sky. Black bush, yucca, mesquite, and mahogany were clothed in garments of fire. Angry embers sang like heated hail, burying in the dry grass of the ponderosa pine flats.

Our hair was white with ash, our faces etched with age.

I had Little Mary pressed against me, shielding her from the blast.

"Which way do we go?" Mary said, as the wall of circling flame drew closer to the river.

With my left hand, I held out the walking stick, and, trembling, it turned downwards. I looked ahead a little ways and saw a gully surrounded by rocks. Built like a fire pit of the gods, it went down deep into the earth. I held the walking stick up again, and it bent towards that bowl of ancientness. We went that way.

Once there, I dug into my medicine bag.

"Whatever I take now, I must use," I told Mary.

I opened my clenched hand.

I had the odd-shaped wrapping of deerskin in which, I knew, there was that reddish war paint. Of what use in the terrible firestorm?

Nonetheless, I opened it, held it in my palm, begging our good friend *Niltsi*, "Little Wind," to guide it on its way.

Now, there rose a playful breeze—*zwoom*—it took the red dust away. The bluish air shifted; the firestorm backed off.

The gaming wind drove it further out into the prairie. There the flames went this way and that, wrestling with an unseen foe. All the while, a lavender mist closed over the land and the sky sparkled with pale raindrops.

And the rust rain came down hard.

A rain of beginnings, a rain from the first days of earth. The tall pine trees were suddenly gushing forth wetness. Out in the prairie, the firestorm danced to a hissing, hunched-down death. Sparks seethed trying desperately to rise, but the red rain put an end to them.

"Thank you, *Niltsi*," I said as we splashed through the falling water.

And then four black horses, four black riders came out of the quivering sky. Four ghostly *chindi* riders, galloping on ghostly *chindi* horses, crashing out of the clouds. And plunging down upon us.

The Medicine Bag Is Deep

As the riders of the storm pounded down, we climbed out of the pit of the gods. We ran just ahead of the great doom shapes overhead. Little Mary cried out as the night-forms came after us. I gave the cradleboard back to Mary, who held it close, as she ran. In another moment, the dark riders with flying, flowing capes were almost on top of us. I saw their horses pawing the air, crashing across the tops of the trees. And I felt their hot breath on my neck and back.

"Use the bag again, Tobachischin," Mary said.

Putting my hand into it, I brought out the horsehair whip.

I had no idea whom to ask; I couldn't beg *Niltsi's* aid again, so I said, "Grandfather, with this . . . draw away their power."

The winds whined. The sky flickered. Roots of lightning criss-crossed. I jabbed my hand out, offering the horsehair whip. It was quickly taken away, and off, and upward, *shhiiffit*!

Now the horsemen, flailing their mounts down the treetops, descended into our midst. Yet, as they neared where we stood in the tumult of rain, something—some force—threw them off balance. The horses whirled out of control; the riders fell.

Something far greater than they was scattering them to the four directions.

"I fear they'll be back." Mary said, watching the riders and their mounts careen away.

As she spoke the rain stopped. The foggy ponderosas dripped, steamed. The violence was gone from the air, the sky, the trees. The forest seemed to have awakened from a nightmare.

"Your grandfather's medicine bag has much power," Mary said, awed.

I wiped my wet face. My ribs were sore from the running, but my sandals were firm and good and I knew if I had to, I could run until dawn. My hand burrowed again into the rain-soaked medicine bag. It retrieved the stone arrow straightener. The tool was shaped like a curved knife with a notch in the center where the new arrow was shaped. I'd seen Grandfather work it, scrubbing the shaft until it was smooth, and worthy of flight.

"May we be blessed with an arrow's speed." I spoke into the rain-broken sky and the arrow straightener was whisked away in a sudden wind. Lightning knotted, flared, ghosted, and was gone. The night sky filled with shimmering starlight.

We were now in a different place. The moon brightened our path. We were perched on a rock ledge, behind which was the mouth of a cave.

Was this our sanctuary in the Lukachukai? That place where *hozhoni* was always present?

"Thank you, Grandfather," I whispered. For I felt him within me, his strength, his appreciation of all things.

And I saw Mary and felt her goodness, too. And Little Mary, her precious sweetness. We went into the cave and built a fire with wood put there by some ancient one. The walls of the cave turned yellow when the tender flame grew, and we saw on the rock walls the carved figures of two-leggeds, animal people, and gods. A sacred place this was. A holy shelter watched over by the unseen presences of the mountain. We gave thanks and Mary fed Little Mary another mouth-moistened stick of deer jerky. And that was all we had, but it was enough to quiet her and while the fire warmed us, we watched the stars dance.

When Little Mary was asleep, Mary whispered to me, "Did you see how far up we are?"

I smiled and touched my hand to her cheek.

Her face was soft as a butterfly's wing. She returned the gesture, then she held my hand in hers. We lay like that for a while, our hands enmeshed, our faces close.

"They almost had us," Mary sighed.

"You mean . . . *he* almost had us."

"I know."

"Were you afraid?"

"Yes."

She squeezed my hand and put her cheek against mine.

"What do we do now?"

"Do not worry," I said softly into her ear. "Grandfather's medicine bag is deep."

However, I knew, far better than she, that the only magic we had left was the porcupine comb and the little blue coyote bead.

Horns with Hawks' Heads

I woke hearing the gray-head song of the nuthatch. Grandfather used to say, "When you hear that bird, rise up, for he is the mischief-maker who turned The People's hair white, and made us grow old before our time." Mary and Little Mary were still asleep. I rose and stepped outside the cave. The sun was just about to rise.

Kneeling, I sang the Dawn Song.

In the house made of dawn, made of pollen, made of
*   dark mist and woman's rain.*
In the house made of grasshoppers and crystals and
*   zigzag lightning.*
With shirt of darkness, come.
Roots of great corn, I shall regain my power. Sprinkling
*   corn pollen have I made my sacrifice. With*
*   headdress and thunder, come soaring.*

With male rain and female rain and with rainbowed
> *wings come soaring, come soaring, come soaring.*
My body restore for me, my mind restore. Happily I
> *walk, happily I hear, happily I step clear of*
> *things done to me.*
Happily my limbs regain their power.
Floating over the rivers of white corn, blue corn, yellow
> *corn, fair corn to the ends of the earth.*
Join me and give me strength for this coming day.
With beauty before me, I walk
With beauty behind me, I walk
With beauty below me, I walk
With beauty above me, I walk
In beauty it is finished
In beauty it is finished
In beauty it is finished
In beauty it is finished.

When I ended my song, I felt strong. In the sunlight I felt the old wound in my leg fade. In the strong sun I felt my ribs turn to iron. I breathed the sun through my left nostril, then through my right nostril, and in the sunlit circle of life, I felt my power grow and enter my bloodstream and fill my bones with light.

I said aloud, "I am ready, Two Face. Do you hear me? I am ready to meet you."

The wind whined in the high pines. I glanced down, wondering how the three of us would get off the cliff, and then remembered my medicine bag. I went inside and got it. Retrieving the porcupine quill comb, I raised it level with the pine tops and holding it aloft, said, "Take this, Sun Father, bring us down to Mother Earth." No sooner had I spoken these words than the comb was flung from my hand—*swweeng*—and end over end, disappeared in the air. At the same time, a great ponderosa bent over against the cliff face.

Mary appeared beside me.

"What was that?"

"Look, Mary, a ladder to the ground."

The great shaggy tree had lodged itself a few hands away from our ledge. There were enough branches to climb down to the forest.

Mary smiled. "Have you used the last of the magic?"

I tapped my fist over my heart four times.

"It is in me now," I replied with confidence. Then I told her, "We still have the blue coyote bead. And if I can only find the white one that goes with it, Two Face will have nothing on us. I am ready to meet him now. This day we shall see whose strength is greater."

We got the rest of our things. I carried the cradleboard and we descended, and then set out on our way. The walking stick showed us tracks. Footprints of that gracious old fellow of the feather woods, Grandfather Turkey. It was he, *Dineh* say, who brought the seeds of life into this world. No bird person—not even Eagle—has more power or wisdom than Turkey Old Man, as we often call him. Nor do any of the winged ones possess more magic than this great grandfather of the first days of life.

"Old One," I said, "You have the gray mist of magic in your feathers. You have the corn of many colors that dazzles the eye. You have the barred feather and the rain beard that bring wisdom. You have the footprints of faith; long have I wanted to see you and ask for your help."

This was my prayer.

Then, in the gabbling fern brake, I heard the noise of that very old grandfather. I heard him, yet he stayed concealed. I motioned to Mary that she should wait for me, and I returned the cradleboard with Little Mary in it. Then I stepped into the soaking fern brake.

I hoped to see Turkey Old Man there on the other side of the pale ferns, but instead there came a trampling sound, a pounding of hooves. A startled doe jumped in front of me. A great buck followed her, eyes gazing calmly in my direction as he walked, high-horned, through the bushes. His antlers were enormous and perched on every point there were birds that I didn't recognize. Red, blue, yellow, black, and green birds.

A queer glare came from the buck's eyes. I blinked—just once—and there was Two Face where the great buck had been. His eyes bore into me, the left one cloudy blue, the right one deeply black. Both eyes, however, seemed to give off a gold-green light, like the crack of the sun before it goes down at dusk.

I was unafraid. I waited. And wondered. This was no mortal man.

"How do you like my home?" he asked gently. As he spoke the ragged scar that forked across his severed face moved as if alive. He seemed so unreal, yet here he was, a man of flesh and bone.

"I like the forest," I said. "It is becoming my home."

"I see," he answered, faintly smiling. Then, "I hadn't believed you were so young, so green. Like this, the forest," and he gestured with his open hand.

I felt my heart leap.

"Is that so?"

"I see you looking at me as if I were deformed. Am I not what you expected? Am I not like my name, Two Face?"

My right hand rested on the handle of my obsidian knife. His good eye saw this, noted it. I crossed my arms like his and let my shoulders sag as if I were as easy in my bones as he was.

"You are more than I expected," I told him, then paused and added, ". . . and less."

His eyes flickered with interest and his lips narrowed. He let out a little snort, laughed derisively. Then he shifted his position, letting his hands drop to his sides. When I looked into his face again, he was smiling crookedly.

I saw what he wore. He had beautifully embroidered moccasins, fringed leggings. His shirt-front was decorated with quill. On his shoulder there was a cape of coyote fur. The head of the coyote was propped over his left shoulder and there were dead holes where the eyes had been. I could see that, when need be, he wore the skin over his head, and the eyes would then come alive.

Two Face caught me staring.

"Friend," he said falsely. "Would you like to wear my coyote robe?"

I decided to play with him.

"What must I do to wear it?"

Two Face grinned. His scar writhed like a gray snake. He came closer.

"There is one thing . . . if you wish to wear and to gain coyote power."

I looked him in the good eye. "And it is?"

"Let me see the medicine bag that you carry on your shoulder, and I will let you have the robe." He slid the coyote's husk off his shoulder and held it to me. It smelled strongly of coyote urine.

I slipped the bag off my shoulder, yet withheld it from him. He stood there with the coyote head extended. He and the dead coyote grinned the same, crookedly.

"Is there something, in particular, that you want?" I peered mockingly into my medicine bag. "Nothing's left, it's all spent."

Two Face's scar tightened. His smile went away.

Grimly, he said, "Be warned, youngster, you are speaking to your elder."

"An elder who gives away his medicine is like a foolish child."

He snorted, then quickly recovered himself.

"I had the same youthful spirit when I was your age." He grinned broadly, unevenly, his face cracking in half.

Shrugging, I said, "I have a little blue bead that can defeat you any time I wish. What have you got that I haven't? Will you turn into a big tame deer with tiny birds in his horns?"

The heavy lid over the blank, sightless milk-eye fluttered, as if trying to take flight. So, too, did the scar curve like a snake.

"What gives you—a mere youth—such brazen confidence? I could crush you as you stand there, and you know it." He gestured with pointed finger, the sign of war.

"As much as you want what I have, you'll not get it, Two Face. The bead is mine and only I know its power." I let my shoulders sag a little more, glancing away, as if I were tired of looking at him.

At that moment, a cold shadow dropped over me, as of a huge bird.

"Are you confident that you will see the sun go behind the mountain?" He pinned me with his dark eye.

I held my ground even though I felt the presence of that ominous bird-shadow hanging over me.

"The bead is mine. No one, living or dead, can take it from me. So my grandfather said, so I know to be true."

"That one whose spirit I sent North—that weak old man?"

My heart leaped at this; my blood burned; yet I remained calm.

The winged thing, the shadow, came coolly down and the ground on which I stood darkened. I breathed deeply, forcing myself not to be angry or crazed, for then I should lose my strength, my will. The shadow lifted. But I felt it settle near us, waiting like an invisible vulture.

"He, the one you speak of, has not gone to the North yet. He stays. Even now I feel him watching."

I saw that this remark had a good effect.

I glanced at him and he turned deliberately and stared into the forest, as if calling for someone, or something with his mind.

Then I saw that great buck stepping among the dripping ferns. On his horn tips the little birds were changed to a hundred red-eyed hawks.

It Is Done, Said the Old One

After Two Face had gone I slung the medicine bag around my neck. There was nothing in it now but the coyote bead.

I knelt and whispered, "Come, Old Man, I have need of you."

And there came the sound of a handful of pebbles being shaken in a hollow gourd.

That rattling seemed to come from everywhere at once.

"Old Man, is that you?"

Rustle of feathers, bristle of wings.

Then, in front of me sitting on a fallen tree, a very old man with white locks hanging down. Brown and white feathers dangled from his frost-like hair. Shriveled like an apple too long in the sun, his face was deeply wrinkled. On either side of his upper lip, he had a thin wispy

127

mustache. He wore a dusty coat of feathers, of the drab kind he had in his hair. The tips of these feathers were snow-white, and I remembered the old song Grandfather taught me when I was a little boy.

> *As the waters rise*
> *The animal people*
> *Climb into two reeds*
> *Turkey Old Man*
> *The last to get into*
> *His reed—the foamy waters*
> *Of the great flood*
> *Whiten the tips of his tail feathers*
> *They are white to this day*
> *Turkey savior, bless this life I live*
> *This bounty I receive*
> *Turkey Old Man*
> *Keep us well*
> *With your gracious seeds of life.*

Turkey Old Man wore a misty mustache and he blinked curiously with his little amber eyes, and the soft, loose folds of skin under his neck jiggled when he nodded, which was often. Every now and then, his head dropped onto his breast and his face disappeared into the ruffles of his dusty coat.

"How are you, Old Man?"

He cackled. "I am well."

"Will you help me?" I asked.

He blinked. "What is it you want, Grandchild?"

I took the medicine bag from my shoulder. Feeling inside for the coyote bead parcel, I found it, then I showed the little blue bead to the old man.

In my open palm the bead gleamed with a wintry glow.

Turkey Old Man gabbled appreciatively, "Ah-hah." He shook all over, his laughter making a pebbly clatter. The trees shivered, but there was no wind. The sun glowed on the blue bead, yet the sun was behind a cloud. Then the old one took two steps, three steps, four. He put out his ancient, scaled hand with long, curved, black fingernails. Cackling, he seized the bead. And it came to life. It jumped out of his clutches and rolled away on the ground.

Turkey Old Man coughed and laughed.

I ran after the bead—but too late. It rolled into an ant's nest, and went—*poot!*—down the hole.

"My bead!"

"*Shushh!*" chortled Turkey Old Man.

I showed him how upset I was.

Of course, he meant no harm. And I knew well that he often played the part of the clown. I remembered this, yet the bead was gone. My only hope to overcome Two Face. Then Turkey Old Man said, "Grandson, do you know the ant chant?"

I nodded. "Is this another crazy trick, Old Man?"

"Life's the trick," he cackled. "You know that by now."

He burst out laughing and the trees bent in the laughing wind.

I was sitting cross-legged in front of the old man.

"Are you going to help me get my bead back?"

He chuckled, "Sing the ant chant, and you'll see something happen."

So I sang the song.

> *Black ant people, by your sense of smell, come out*
> *Put together what has been taken apart*
> *Black ant people, I sing this song*
> *Praying and singing, I sing this song*

So that you will know I mean well
So that you will put together what has been put asunder
Black ant people, by your sense of smell
Grant us your goodness.

I was seated before the anthill, singing, and Turkey Old Man was standing on one foot, then the other, listening.

When I was finished he scolded me.

"You sing without feeling," he chided.

"I sing the best I can," I protested.

He cackled and shook his great dusty brown coat until pinfeathers floated like tufts of snow. His wrinkled, red-apple face was vexed.

"All right. I'll sing it again—"

"Do it with heart," he urged.

I said I would do that, and then I sang the ant chant again, this time putting my whole being into it.

When I was done, he came at me again. The skin under his chin was wattled; it shook as he spoke.

"You forgot to ask them to bring the blue bead together with the white one. These beads have been apart for a long time. Tell the black ant people this—but put it in your words."

I did this thing, just the way he wanted me to, and when I was through singing, he exhaled loudly, and I thought, approvingly.

Then I looked at the anthill and there on the side of the mound were two beads: blue and white, side by side. I took them and put them into my medicine bag.

"Done," the old one said, sighing.

We heard a coyote howl four times. On the fourth cry, four bear men came out of the bracken, claws clicking, teeth dripping. They were big Utes, swaddled in heavy black bearskins. Their flesh underneath the furs was darkened with clay and their teeth were long and sharp and stuck out of their lips.

I hoped the old one would do something, but he now walked off into the bushes, gobbling. I was alone.

The bears closed in.

The Long Walk Home

These were the same men who'd killed the woman at the sheep camp. They were the riders of the fire storm night . . . further phantoms sent by a sorcerer who rarely did his own bidding. The Utes had bloody scalps on their belts and they lumbered over to the log where Turkey Old Man had been, and I noticed their necks were ringed with claws, and their furious bear's eyes bore into me.

"You want the beads?" I asked, pretending to dig into my medicine bag.

They showed me—all four at once—their greasy, gray upper teeth.

"Very well," I said, "you shall have them."

Taking the two beads out into the light, I dropped them, one at a time, into a crack in the log. In the forest there came a gabbling and a gobbling. Somehow, I knew the old one hadn't abandoned me; he was still somewhere near.

The bear men attacked the crack, their claws ripping at the bark.

"I'll help," I offered. Drawing my obsidian knife, I buried it like a wedge in the crack and then I got a heavy, round rock and began to pound the knife deeper in. The crack widened, splintered open.

"Get your hands as far in as you can and pry with all your might."

Growling, they clawed to the task. Their necklaces of claws jingled, their grunts filled the small clearing. I pounded the knife as far as it would go.

"Get your fingers farther in," I told them, and they did. They buried them to their wrists.

"Let the strongest pull hardest!"

They obeyed and their hands were swallowed into the split log, whereupon, I knocked my knife with the rock and it spun out of the log and fell on the ground. At the same time, the crack closed; fingers trapped, the Utes roared.

The woods rang with their pain. I got up from the log, stepped back, and picked up Grandfather's walking stick. Taking the narrow tip in my hands, I swung it like a club.

The bear men began to fall over themselves, trying to get away. Failing to do this, they dragged the log and clumped off in a crippled fashion. I came after them, swinging the walking stick at their heads. Four blows I delivered, dropping each of the bear men on the ground, dead. As they slumped over, their shadows fled from them. The dark clay on their skin cracked. Their bear capes dried up and turned into black dust.

Naked they lay. Then flesh and bone. Then nothing.

A loud gabbling told me the old one was back again.

He stood next to me, nodding.

"Nice," he said. "Nicely done."

He caught me with his hand. "Do not forget to get those beads out of the log."

"Those were just glass beads I got off my shirt," I told him. "I have the real ones in the bag."

A coyote call shattered the stillness.

"He waits for you," said the old one.

Then came Mary's voice—screaming.

I tore through the ferns, running to help her.

She was standing where I'd left her. Beside her was a dark, shaggy coyote man.

"Do you really think you can do anything—to *me*?"

It was Two Face speaking through his ugly mask of fur. His eyes were yellow; gold smoke slipped from his lips as he spoke.

"You have no power over me," I warned. "I have the beads."

Grabbing Mary's hand, he twisted it roughly behind her. He kept twisting until she crumpled to her knees.

I reached for my knife, remembered where it lay in the clearing, and stood there, helpless.

Two Face grinned, his coyote fangs showing. His face and the mask were one and his gold eyes glowed bright when he talked and dimmed when he didn't.

"You're both dead," he said, eyes aglow.

His voice crackled.

Mary writhed as Two Face twisted her arm. Little Mary, lying in her cradleboard, was crying fitfully. I didn't know what to do. I stood by, fists clenched, heart pounding with indecision.

"I'll smash the baby," he said, his lips curling, revealing yellow fangs.

Two Face raised his furred hand to cast a spell, but a sudden pebble-shaking noise startled him. The woods rattled, the trees shook, the disturbing noise, as of an army of cicadas, increased in volume.

"What's this?" Two Face exclaimed, his clawed hand frozen in midair.

Turkey Old Man stumbled out of the bushes, his feather coat all askew. He stood bony and brown in the sun, his chins sagging, his knees knocking.

"Old fool, what can you do?" Two Face mocked.

Turkey Old Man said nothing, but he took off his brown dusty coat and dropped it on the ground. Suddenly, it moved, it jumped, it barked. And it dragged itself over to where I was.

Two Face stared, outraged.

"I still have powers," the old one laughed.

"I'll wring your neck," Two Face said as he cast Mary aside. She ran for the cradleboard and picked up Little Mary.

Two Face paid her no mind. He took four steps towards Turkey Old Man, raised his furred hands, and shot zigzag lightning from his claws. Eight jagged bolts buried themselves into the old one.

He blossomed into flame. And, like a bag of burning pinfeathers, he blew away.

Two Face cried out in triumph; his sap-colored eyes oozed yellow smoke. He came for me.

A wind rustled in the woods; the feather coat was torn away—in its place were two coyote pups. The female was white, the male was blue.

Two Face, seeing them at the same time I did, raised his lightning claws, but before he could throw zigzag fire, I put a blue bead into the mouth of the male pup and a white bead into the female pup.

A soft rain fell. A rainbow glittered. Turkey Old Man's laughter made the woods ring with pebbles.

Two Face, however, leaked yellow smoke as the rain

melted him. A buck with hawk's heads on its antlers flashed briefly before our eyes, faded. Four bears pawed the air, dissolved. Four black horses whinnied and waned and two messengers, one tall and one short, gleamed, empty-faced, before they, too, disappeared.

The rainbow stayed.

The rain rained.

Mary pressed Little Mary between us, saying, "It's over."

The two coyote pups yipped.

The woods cackled.

We gathered our things for the long walk home.

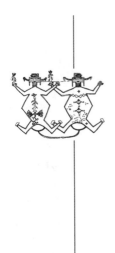

Our Life as One

A man and woman are married in the old way.

The man, Tobachischin; the woman, Mary.

Here in the mountains, they call me "He-Who-Al-ways-Wins." Mary is called "With-Wind-She-Runs." There are about two hundred *Dineh* in hiding. Living in secrecy. How did we find this closed canyon in the midst of the mountains?

One day, Mary and I followed a wild horse with a mad mooneye, and it happened that the horse wasn't wild, but part of a hidden herd. As the horses grazed on the tall mountain grass, we saw a Navajo herdsman. He had goats and sheep as well as horses. His name, he told us that day, was Goats. And he brought us to the leader of this renegade band of *Dineh* living in the Lukachukai, their hidden home.

Thus did our new life begin, far from *Hweeldi* where the rest of our defeated nation remained imprisoned, their spirits broken.

The way we were married in the old way went like this; it was like the dream I had in the desert while we were running away. Yet, this time, I was the one in Mary's favor . . . not the coyote man, Two Face.

On our marriage day before the first light of the sun touched our hands, I dipped water from a sacred water jar, and poured it over the hands of my bride. Then the wedding basket was passed round to the small gathering of friends. When it came to me, I took a fingerful of cornmeal mush from the east, the south, the west, the north, and lastly, the center (never the center first, as in the bad dream). After this Mary received the basket and did the same.

Then came the time for the wedding race: this was to the river and back again; not a long run but a very short one.

I started out strong, pretending by the time I reached the river, some one hundred yards off, to tire and to grow weak. Mary arrived at the riverbank ahead of me. Thus she is the one who will bring riches to our family. That is our way, our custom. We have only each other and Little Mary. Yet one day we will have all the bounty that *hozhoni* provides. All blessings flow from Changing Woman. She is the beginning and the end; it starts with her, it ends with her.

At our marriage no horses were given to the bride's parents—we have no parents, we have no horses. However, those who have come to make us feel welcome are all the family we need. They are The People who survived four hard, lonely, canyon-walled winters. They are the mountain-hidden-few, who refused The Long Walk to *Hweeldi*. Like us they stayed, like us they lived.

For it is said in The Coyote Bead Ceremony, "The two shall become one."

About the Author

Gerald Hausman traces his immediate roots to Hungarian Jews and Gypsies on his father's side and English and Algonquian descendants on his mother's. He is related to California gold seekers, bear hunters, maritime mercenaries, and members of the first family married at Plymouth in 1633. He discovered a Seminole kinsman who worked his way free of indentured servitude to become a wealthy New England landholder. Mr. Hausman's twenty-two years among the Navajo are fully reflected in his books about The People, who have honored him by broadcasting his version of their creation stories on Navajo radio. One of these stories, "Turquoise Horse," was recently selected by The Great Books Foundation for an audiology anthology.

Hampton Roads Publishing Company

. . . for the evolving human spirit

Hampton Roads Publishing Company
publishes books on a variety of subjects including
metaphysics, health, complementary medicine,
visionary fiction, and other related topics.

For a copy of our latest catalog,
call toll-free, 800-766-8009,
or send your name and address to:

Hampton Roads Publishing Company, Inc.
134 Burgess Lane
Charlottesville, VA 22902
e-mail: hrpc@hrpub.com
www.hrpub.com